Sins of the Fathers

Judith Liebaert

D1169454

Tellectual Press
tellectual.com

Tellectual Press
tellectual.com
Valley, WA

Print ISBN: 978-1-942897-10-1

Tellectual Press is an imprint of Tellectual LLC.

The cover image was composed by Edwin A. Suominen with the free GIMP image processing software, based on a photograph taken by Michael Grubbs of a pocket knife in his collection. Permission for use in the image composition is gratefully acknowledged. Michael purchased this beautiful knife from his barber Danny ("a class act with genuine character") after one of his frequent haircuts while serving in the U.S. Coast Guard.

Table of Contents

For my mentor and friend
Catherine "Kay" Coletta

I

Cases that have been cold for decades are often solved in one of two ways: either with a confession or by a similar crime with the same signature.

—Edward Anderson,
Detective Sgt., Douglas County Sheriff's Dept. (ret.),
Past president, Wisconsin Assoc. of Homicide Investigators

I never meant to kill anyone. That was a choice made for me a long time ago, but how could I possibly explain it?

I first saw the boy when I drove past Immaculate Heart one day, on my way to buy groceries at the Super One. He looked to be about twelve or thirteen years old. He was doing yard work around the rectory, mowing and raking. I saw him again the next day, cleaning up the old shed and hauling boxes of trash to the curb. I started making a point to drive past the church every day. Sometimes I parked in the shadows of the trees along the street.

I was watching him the day he found the knife. He came out of the shed into the bright sunlight, turning it over in his small hands, wiping the grime off it with the bottom edge of his t-shirt. When I realized what he was holding I couldn't believe it myself. It was right there all these years and nobody else had ever found it. How could that be possible?

He pulled the blade out of the handle, admiring it, brushing his finger along its edge. Spit polished the steel. Held it up to the sun. I knew exactly what he was feeling.

After that I tried to stay away, to get the crazy idea I was cooking up out of my head. What did I have to worry about, anyway? He probably didn't even know what he had or how it could ruin me, but it was no use, I couldn't stop thinking about him or the knife. I couldn't stop watching him.

I saw his friends hanging around a couple of times, at least I figured they were his friends. Most of them looked older and they seemed to tease him a lot. I think that's why he showed them the knife. He hoped it would impress them.

I knew I was in trouble after that, no matter what I did. That's when I came up with my plan. I went over it in my head, how I would just start up a conversation with him, then gain his confidence, sweet talk him a little before offering to buy the knife off of him. I'd make it worth it, fifty or even a hundred bucks, whatever it took. Little went as I had planned, however.

That day I approached him he was working on the hedge around the rectory yard. He was about halfway done clipping the long row of shrubbery that separated the two-story brick building from the sidewalk. He was past the spot where the hedge turns a corner to run along the side yard, before ending at the parking lot. It was back from the street. There was only one window on that side of the rectory and the shades were drawn, just like always. If anybody was inside, they wouldn't see us.

He looked up as soon as I started talking, even though I was still several feet away on the sidewalk. I said it was a hot day to be clipping hedges. He answered it was hot as hell. I laughed and said that was funny, being that he was working on holy ground. I'd left the sidewalk, moving closer to him until I was standing right across from him with the hedge in between us. We were talking then, having a conversation. It wouldn't look so much like I was a stranger bothering a kid I didn't know.

"So, are you working off penance?" I said, a big fake grin on my face.

"Nope. Just working."

"Doing good deeds then," I said.

"Not exactly." He kept to his task, clipping off errant shoots that rose above the standard, with the rhythmic scraping of steel blades scissoring against one another marking his steady pace. "Father Carmichael asked my mom if I could do some work around the rectory this summer. I guess she thinks it's some kind of sin for an altar boy to say no to a priest, so here I am."

Altar boy. With his golden hair and guileless face he'd look angelic in those white robes, but he was no angel.

"You seem too old to still be an altar boy." He didn't, but kids like it when an adult thinks they're older. I wanted him to like me.

"Yeah, I was confirmed this year—so I don't have to do it anymore."

That surprised me. The kid was older than I thought.

"Sounds like your mom has different ideas. What's your dad think?"

"He ain't around much. Drives truck."

I was carrying a smaller, paper grocery bag by the edge that I'd rolled up into a handle of sorts, the contents carefully selected to fit my plan. I tucked it under one arm and shifted my weight, sliding one foot forward, trying to look nonchalant. "That's tough for you and your mom, I bet."

The boy shrugged his shoulders. "We do okay."

His lethargic clipping became more aggressive. He attacked the shrubbery with a jab and slice motion, with muscles flexing from his neck to his shoulders and down into his slender biceps below his t-shirt sleeves. I realized just then that this kid might be more than I bargained for.

I tried to diffuse his anger. "You're getting paid though, right?"

"Not near enough," he said.

"Still, a fella your age . . . I'll bet you're saving up to buy a car."

"Nope. My mom says I can use my dad's as soon as I get my permit later this year."

So he was fifteen, at least. "Makes sense if it's just sitting around when he's on the road," I said.

He didn't say anything.

"Well, I guess I'd better let you get back to work if you're going to finish before dark." I looked at the sun coming around the west side of the building, cutting an angle of light between the hedge and rectory.

"Should've started earlier," he said. "I thought it might be cooler after supper. Guess I was wrong."

"It's been pretty hot for this early in the summer. It won't last long, though. There's a cold front coming down from Canada. Should hit later tonight." I pulled the bag out from under my arm. "I'd offer you a cold root beer," I said, holding out the bag to indicate its contents. "But I don't have an opener." I pulled one of the bottles from the four-pack in the bag. "Special brew. See?"

I saw his brow wrinkle with a grimace before a heavy fringe of hair dipped down onto his forehead, falling over his eyes. They were the same color as the summer sky. He combed his hair aside with spread fingers and I caught a whiff of clean, unscented soap–old-fashioned, Ivory maybe, from the bathroom sink in the rectory, I guessed.

"I don't drink root beer much. Mom brings home A&W from the drive-in sometimes."

"I like this one," I said. "It has a real bite–perfect for making root beer floats. It doesn't get too mellowed out by the ice cream. You know what I mean? Tastes just like cream soda when that happens."

I'd never tasted the stuff in the bag. They stocked it at the gas station out on East Second Street at a hefty price for the tourists. I just wanted something cold and tempting enough. Something without a twist-off cap.

"Yeah, I guess," he said.

"Well, you probably wouldn't care for it anyway. It's pretty strong."

"I can open it." He set the clippers down on the grass and reached into his pocket, pulling out the knife.

I handed him a bottle and he popped the cap off with the serrated part of the blade, like I figured he would. "Think I'll join you," I said, holding out a second bottle. He passed me the first one, then opened the second one and took a big swig before folding the knife and dropping it into the pocket of his baggy cargo shorts.

"Pretty cool knife," I said. "My dad gave me one when I was just about your age. I lost it though." I took another swallow from the bottle. "You buy it with the money you're earning?"

He took a swig of root beer instead of answering. We both drank for a while until I said I'd better get going again. He formed his mouth around the lip of the bottle and chugged the rest of the contents without stopping, then he handed me the empty.

"Yeah," he said, before he burped without shame. "I sure don't want to have to come back tomorrow to finish this."

"That knife—you know how to sharpen the blade?"

He bent down to pick up the hedge clipper. "Yup."

I pushed things a little more. "It's a real skill. You can ruin it if you do it wrong."

He just looked at me. I was bothering him now. "Sure. And it's sharp enough now," he said. "Real sharp, as a matter of fact."

It occurred to me he hadn't even said thank you for the root beer. That irked me. He had a hard edge I hadn't planned on. It threw me off my game. "You worried I'm going to steal it off you or something?" I asked.

He smirked, looking me up and down. "I ain't worried about that."

"So what's your deal?"

"No *deal*. It's mine and I don't have to show it to some crazy old man. Now get outta here and leave me alone."

Crazy old man. So I wouldn't be winning him over—that much was sure. "I know all about that knife," I said. "More than you think. I saw you showing it off to your friends."

"So what?"

"I know it has a name engraved on it, and the name isn't yours."

The boy backed up a step.

The confident sneer faded and the color drained from his face. "How'd you know there's a name on it?" he said.

I saw clouds of fear drifting into his eyes. He knew the significance of the name. He was scared now, but not scared enough to keep his mouth shut. I had to change that.

I reached over the hedge and grabbed him by the front of his shirt before he could take another step back. I felt the panic coming off him in hot, sweaty waves. The stink of his perspiration overpowered the soap I'd smelled on his hands. "Just give it back to me, and I won't haul your ass into that rectory and tell the first priest I see that you have it. Then you can try to explain *why* you have it. After that, there's the matter of possessing evidence in an open murder case." I was making it up as I went along, but what would the kid know?

"You're a cop?"

Did I want him to think so? If it would get him to hand over the knife, I did. "That's right kid, and I've been watching you. You're in more trouble than you want to know."

The boy tugged at his shirt, trying to free it from my grip "If you're a cop, where's your badge? Why didn't you just show it to me, and ask me for the knife?"

The kid was smart. I started dragging him toward the walkway and the front of the rectory with the hedge still between us, making up new lies as I went along. "Listen kid, I'm not a cop. I'm a private detective. Now, we can do this the hard way, or we can do it the easy way. The hard way is up the front steps and in the door of the rectory. Then the police *will* get involved.

He tried yanking himself back, and I grabbed more shirt into my fingers, tightening it around his neck. "The easy way, kid, is you giving me that knife. Then all this will just be our little secret."

I pulled him the last foot or so toward the walkway up to the rectory steps. The hedge no longer separated us. I yanked him close, getting right up to his face, boring into his eyes with my own. "Gimme the knife, kid." I reached down into his pocket, the one he'd put the knife back in.

"Lemme go, you fucking perve!" he yelled, jerking his hips around to get away.

His voice was loud, and it wasn't even his best effort yet. If he wanted to, he could bring the whole neighborhood running to his rescue, ready to give a pedophile a beat down. I loosened my grip on his shirt.

He took advantage of my momentary hesitation and came down hard with his fist on my forearm, yanking his t-shirt away at the same time. A runt, but wiry and a lot stronger than I'd expected. He took off in a dead run, darting around the back of the rectory.

I cut through the churchyard and came into the parking lot in time to see him grab his bike from the side of the tool shed where he'd left it leaning. He hopped on and pedaled, fast, up the street.

No way was I going to catch him on foot. Time for the truck. It was parked out of sight in a tight corner formed by the rectory garage and the outcrop of the church that contained the altar apse and sacristy. I ran to it, got in and started it, and then hesitated a second, my foot on the brake, holding the car back. I could just leave, take my chances that he wouldn't tell anybody about the old guy who grabbed him. Or, I could follow him.

———

I saw him ahead of me, turning onto the gravel road along the railroad tracks that run under the viaduct. I couldn't figure why he went that way, but I followed. He kept turning around to see how close I was. Every time he did, his bike wobbled in the loose gravel and he struggled to keep it upright.

The last time, he turned to face forward again too quickly and oversteered the bike. He careened back and forth a few times before going down, taking a header in the gravel not far in front of me.

I stopped my truck and got out.

He was lying crumpled on the ground with one side of his face right down in the gravel. His forehead had a dirty smudge above the temple. A shallow cut in the middle. He'd have a good goose egg popping out soon.

I rolled him onto his back. He was stunned but breathing okay. I fished in his pockets for the knife. All I had to do was take it and leave him there. He didn't know who I was. Maybe the knock on his head would screw with his memory, or be enough to cast doubt on whatever story he told.

Then he started moaning and pushing my hands away. Damn it.

"I know all about the knife, old man," he croaked out from down there in the gravel. "You're the one who killed that Baker kid, you godammn perve. Leave me alone."

Maybe I could've left him there, just drive away. Drive and drive and keep on driving, up into Canada and then just disappear from there. But he could've described me. He could've identified my truck. Even if I'd made it to the border, I'd never have gotten across.

So I got down on my knees, the gravel pushing sharp and deep through my pants, holding the kid as he started to struggle again. I wrapped my right hand behind his head, cupped his jaw in my left. Then I pulled hard and snapped his scrawny neck.

Everything went quiet, just the sound of the gravel shifting and some distant traffic as I got back up and took one last quick look at what I'd done.

Like I said, I never wanted to kill anyone. But what choice did I have?

II

Rita Sullivan wheeled her cream-colored VW bug into the Perkins lot. She looked out at the choppy waves on the bay of Lake Superior. "Definitely not a top-down day, Charlie," she said, patting the dashboard.

She wasn't in the habit of naming her cars, but the moment she'd laid eyes on this one, with its brown top over a light cream body, it reminded her of the ugly saddle shoes Nicholas Cage wore in *Peggy Sue Got Married.* She had been fourteen years old and crush-ready when she saw the movie. Cage's portrayal of the unlikely Romeo, Charlie Bodell, had made her shiver with desire. His bedroom eyes and hip-thrusting rendition of *I Wonder Why* sent her stomach into free fall, the same as a fast downward plunge on a roller coaster, the same as when she met Mark in high school. These days, roller coasters terrified her almost as much as the idea of falling in love.

She cut the engine and slid the seat back, grumbling a few choice words about the inclement weather. She knew her little convertible wasn't the wisest choice in a northern climate, but her reporter's salary at the *Superior Telegram* wasn't near enough to finance her dream car–a gold Jaguar XRK pimped out with a custom, leopard-print rag top. Now that would give people something to look at.

"Don't worry, Charlie." She pulled the keys from the car's ignition. "You're still my guy."

The wind blowing down from Canada and across the cold lake water was a fan aimed over a big bowl of ice. Yesterday's balmy temperatures had plummeted overnight to a cool sixty degrees. Rita dreaded getting out of her car, but she'd bet the bite of that cold wind was going to sting less than Pops's opinion of her latest feature story.

Rita opened the driver's door, holding on tight, fighting against the gale that threatened to rip it from her grasp and slam it into the car parked next to her. The white behemoth dwarfed her little bug. She might not know one SUV from another, but she knew this one was pricey, and she didn't need an outrageous claim filed on her insurance company for a little door ding.

She held her breath, slammed the bug's door shut behind her, ducked her head against the wind and ran for the building, but not before pressing the button on her key twice to make sure the doors were locked. *Thanks Pops,* she thought.

She hurried through the double glass doors into the restaurant. Inside the entry, she tried to smooth her shoulder-length hair and short bangs back into place after all the wind but doubted she'd made any improvement. She wished she would've just tied it back in a ponytail and been done with it, but the carefree style wasn't as flattering as it once was, only drawing attention to the silver strands that had begun streaking through her hair when she was barely thirty-five. Now, almost a decade later, the ribbons of gray at her temples made her look older than she liked.

The hostess smiled at her. "He's waiting for you."

She'd been meeting Pops for breakfast every Sunday since her grandmother died six years ago. He hadn't set foot in Immaculate Heart since the funeral; paying homage to a plate of French toast and sausage was his new religion. Rita found it hard to believe he'd gone to mass all those years just to please Grandma Abby, but there seemed no other explanation. She wondered if there were any such devoted men to be found now, or if they were an extinct breed.

She navigated around the center tables to reach Pops, sitting in a booth along the back wall. "Hi Pops. Sorry I'm late."

"You're right on time," he said. "Besides, I've got all the time in the world."

Pops hadn't been in a hurry since the day he retired, something that wore on Grandma Abby's short patience until the day she died.

Rita reached for the empty mug in front of her and poured the rich, black brew from the pot up to the rim. The coffee was bold and strong; the aroma alone gave her a caffeine rush. There were restaurants in Superior Rita avoided simply because their coffee was too weak for her taste.

"Did you see my story Friday?" She knew Pops still read every edition of the *Telegram* from front to back.

"I did," he said, nodding his head. Then he repositioned the coffee pot, the salt and pepper shakers, the dish of creamers, the knife and fork resting on his napkin.

His OCD tendencies, no matter how slight, irritated Rita, the same way having to push the button twice to lock her car grated on her. She wanted to randomly scatter the items Pops had precisely placed around the table, just to prove she could.

"So, what did you think—of the story?" she asked.

"You know how I feel about that story."

"It's the anniversary, Pops. The paper has to run something about the biggest cold case in Superior's history."

"It's been fifty years since the Baker boy was killed. It's never going to be solved; why keep rehashing it? Killers just get lucky sometimes—there isn't enough evidence, no clear trail left behind."

"But the science has improved, Pops. They've solved other cold cases that were almost as old."

"You're like a dog with a bone, girl. It's time to just bury it and forget it."

"You're the one who said there's always a mistake, always something the killer doesn't think about, something that will trip him up."

"When did I say that?"

"When I was a kid, and we used to watch Columbo and Rockford Files together."

"Oh for Pete's sake, those were TV shows."

"Doesn't matter. You always told me what to watch for and how the criminal was going to get caught. You know I listened to everything you ever said to me."

"Oh, your grandmother and I should have been so lucky," Pops said. He took another drink of coffee, drawing the hot liquid through his pursed lips in a prolonged sip. It was his loud and annoying practice of pulling in air while holding the coffee in his mouth in an attempt to cool it before swallowing.

A waitress appeared at the side of the booth. "What'll it be today?"

"The usual," Pops said.

Every waitress there knew Pops. "Sure thing," she said, flashing him a smile. "French toast, sausage links, orange juice." Then, she looked at Rita, pen poised over her pad.

Rita rambled off her order, anxious to get back to her conversation with Pops.

"Forget whatever I said, and listen to what I'm telling you now," he said, after the girl walked away. "Leave it alone. It's never going to be solved. Thomas Baker's death was an accident. There was no motive because it wasn't premeditated. No motive, no physical evidence leading back to the killer. It's a dead end."

"After all these years, I don't understand why they don't just open the files. There could be something in there, a clue that would make somebody realize they have an important piece of the puzzle—something they didn't think was relevant."

"I don't understand your fascination with this case, Rita."

"It's my job, Pops. It's what I do."

"I thought reporters covered the news. This isn't news anymore."

"I asked a cop at the station if they'd ever re-tested the evidence samples. He said he didn't know. If they did, would it be in the file?"

"You're pestering them down at the station?"

"It's not like you think, Pops. I'm a reporter, not some looney tune with a conspiracy theory." She was well aware of what the cops thought of armchair detectives with half-baked theories, and even more aware of how Pops felt about her behavior reflecting on him.

"Rita, I left the force in '67. I don't know what they have or haven't done with that case."

Pops was the desk sergeant on duty the night Thomas Baker's body was found on the refinery road, after he'd disappeared from the parking lot of Immaculate Heart early that morning. Rita was sure if there were any developments in the case over the last fifty years Pops would know about it, whether he was on or off the force.

The waitress returned with their breakfasts, balancing the large plates all the way up her forearm. Rita always admired the skill. She couldn't carry a bowl of soup to the table without it sloshing over the rim.

"Anything else I can get you?" the girl asked.

"The kitchen sink is about all that's left," Pops said looking at Rita's breakfast selections of eggs Benedict, with bacon instead of ham, American fries on the side and a caramel roll to go.

"Are you food shaming me, Pops?"

"Food shaming?" he asked.

"Trying to make me feel guilty about how much I eat?"

"No, no," he said. He took another sip of his coffee.

"Just say it, Pops. You think I'm getting fat, don't you?"

"Well, I have noticed you're putting on a little weight, from behind."

The Sullivan men liked their women petite. Grandma Abby never weighed more than a hundred pounds fully dressed in winter, including her wool coat and Sorel boots. Rita's mother was a waif, too, judging from the few photos Rita had seen of her. But that, unfortunately, could have been due to addiction as much as genetics.

Rita, standing at five-foot-six, could barely squeeze her derrière into a size ten. There were no two ways about it; she was a throwback to her grandfather's tribe, most of them Bo Hunks from Croatia and the Romanian foothills, all hearty peasant stock. That was about as much as Rita knew of her ancestors.

Pops's parents came to America utterly poor and completely illiterate in English. Given there was never any correspondence with family left back in Europe, she guessed they weren't much better at reading and writing their own language. The Sullivan name was a misnomer, at best guess it was an Americanized version of *Slovaneau* or something close to it. But Sullivan it was on the first child's birth certificate, and so it remained all the way down to Pops–David Michael Sullivan.

"It's okay, Pops. I have a fat ass. I'm learning to live with it."

"Don't say that, Rita."

"Really, it's okay. I've accepted my fate."

"No, I mean the word. Don't say that word. Say butt or hind end."

Rita just smiled. "You've seen all of your sisters, right? They're pretty broad across the hind end."

He grinned. "Good child-bearing hips."

Rita wouldn't know about that.

"I'll probably be eating salad or a bowl of cold cereal for dinner, so I guess the calories all even out at the end of the day." she said. She hadn't cooked much since the divorce. When she did, there was always too much, and she ended up throwing most of it away.

"If you say so," Pops agreed.

She ate a few bites before jumping into the fray again. "Pops, I know that murder still haunts you."

"Homicide. It's a homicide until somebody proves different. It could have been an accident–completely unintentional."

She watched him coat the hot French toast in butter and then drown the two slices in syrup. One good thing about having Pops's genetics, she'd probably be around for a long time. He was pushing eighty-seven but easily passed for a much younger man, despite eating all the wrong things.

"Unintentional? How can you be so sure of that?" Rita asked.

"Leave it alone, Rita."

"The body was dumped on an isolated road. It wasn't the scene of the crime. If it was an accident, why would somebody try to cover it up by moving the body? Why not just report it and tell the truth?"

"People panic. They're afraid they'll be blamed. Self-preservation is a strong instinct, Rita. You can't bring a dead person back to life so the next best thing to do is protect yourself, and hope the truth never comes out."

"You say that like it's an acceptable thing to do."

"No. Not at all. I'm saying that's what a desperate, innocent man might do."

"Why cover his head? It might not have been common knowledge fifty years ago. But now every profiler worth his tin badge knows that points to somebody the victim knew, right?"

Pops's eyes never left the plate of French toast. He spoke between mouthfuls. "Maybe. Or it was somebody who couldn't bear to see what they'd done, even to a stranger. I don't know, Rita."

After years of getting the story, Rita knew how to read people. She didn't miss the nuance in Pops's voice, the change in tone, the almost imperceptible rise in volume when he admitted he didn't know. It was a personal failure, in his estimation.

"Is it true they always keep some detail of the murder from the press?" she asked.

"It's a method of investigation, yes."

"Was it knife wounds? There was never a single thing in the paper about any cuts or stab wounds, but there was an all-out manhunt for Thomas Baker's folding knife. Why, Pops?"

"Geeze, don't you ever give up?" Pops put his fork down and pushed his plate away, his breakfast only half eaten. "You're letting your imagination get away with you. They were looking for the knife simply because he was known to always carry it with him. It wasn't found with his body. Whoever had it, or has it, would be a prime suspect."

"Then why would anybody take the knife, or keep it for that matter? Especially if it's a free ticket to jail?"

"Souvenir."

"Then you *don't* believe it was an accident?"

"You asked why. I'm just giving you one reason somebody might do that." Pops sighed. "Brigitta, why do you have to spoil a nice meal with such an unpleasant subject?"

He used her full name. He was getting impatient with her.

"One report said Thomas Baker's clothes were being sent to a crime lab in Madison. Another one said his clothes were kept at the police station for evidence."

"Well of course they kept them there," he explained. "Until they made the decision to send them to the crime lab, or after they were returned."

"In less than a week?"

"Crime labs weren't what they are now, there was only so much testing they could do—and they weren't backlogged like they are today."

"What about the report of a tan car seen parked near the church early that morning?"

"Dead end. Just like every other tip that came in. Gee whiz, Rita, why do you have to ask me all of this?"

"Who else am I going to ask?"

"Why are you asking at all?" Pops questioned.

"Maybe I always wanted to carry on the family tradition. Maybe I should have been a detective." Rita tapped her index finger on her chin just below her mouth.

Pops took his napkin from his lap and dabbed at the teardrop of syrup on his chin. "Detective, right." He scoffed, "I was the only cop in the family and for only sixteen years. That's hardly a tradition."

He stabbed a piece of French toast with his fork and pushed it around the plate, soaking up syrup. "Took me years to get that master's degree. What about that tradition?"

"Educational counseling? Can you just see me dealing with a bunch of high school teenagers every day? Sorry, Pops, not my bag."

"Kids aren't as bad as you think."

"Pops, I don't think kids are bad—" She stopped mid-sentence. "Never mind."

"And I worked in job placement with veterans, not high school kids." Pops filled his mouth again, but not before letting out an exasperated humph of breath.

Rita ignored him. "Pops, I've read every article ever written on this case and not one of them ever mentioned results from the crime lab. What did the police file say?"

"You expect me to remember that after all this time? If it was anything important, the case wouldn't have gone cold."

"Come on, Pops. You remember every detail. Is that what was held back from the press—the results from the crime lab?"

"I'm telling you I don't remember. It was fifty years ago. I'm an old man."

It was Rita's turn to scoff. "Don't try to pull that feeble minded hustle on me. You're still sharp as a tack."

Pops grinned.

"There was only one mention in the newspaper about possible molestation," Rita said. "The medical examiner ruled it out because the body was found fully dressed and his clothes were all intact."

"Yes, that makes sense."

"Really? Are you sure, Pops?"

Rita's knew her grandfather hadn't lived such a sheltered life, but he always played the prude around her.

"Because it's a pretty weak conclusion, if you ask me," Rita said. "He was abducted early in the morning, and they didn't find him until that night. A lot can happen in twelve hours."

Pops's eyebrows squirmed up and down like two fuzzy gray caterpillars on his forehead. He took his napkin from his lap and put it on the table with great purpose, a white flag for her to see.

"Rita, I'm going to the men's room. When I get back, I don't want to talk about this anymore."

Rita watched her grandfather walk away, a slight limp in his step from skipping the physical therapy after hip surgery. It left him with one leg slightly shorter than the other and no sympathy from Grandma Abby.

She'd harped her admonition at her stubborn husband so often Rita still heard it every time she watched Pops walk with his crooked little gait. *If you'd kept up with your therapy, you wouldn't be limping. Now you'll need a lift in your shoe.* May as well tell Pops to cut an inch off one leg; no way was he going to wear a lift.

Rita looked at the half-eaten French toast and lone sausage link getting cold in the puddle of congealed butter and syrup. Pops never liked cooking for himself after Grandma passed. He relished every meal not prepared by his own hands.

Great, now his Sunday breakfast is getting cold.

She pushed the last forkful of egg and English muffin around her plate to sop up every bit of hollandaise sauce. It looked like she'd licked the plate by the time she was finished. Pops was right; she had an unhealthy relationship with food.

She leaned back in the booth and sipped her coffee, mulling over what her grandfather said about the missing knife. Could a kid have killed the Baker boy? The possibility caused a blip of activity in the case a few years after it went cold. Charlie Heck, punk kid, typical bully, not too smart—went around telling kids he'd kill them the same way he killed the Baker boy. It bought him a ticket to the inside of an interrogation room, but nothing ever came of it.

When Pops returned to their booth, he pushed his plate aside, centered his cup in front of him and poured more coffee from the plate.

"Aren't you going to finish your breakfast?"

"No. I've lost my appetite."

"Because of me?" She felt the words catch in her throat. "Oh, Pops, I'm sorry. I just can't stop thinking about this case."

Rita wondered if she would ever get over these sudden and overwhelming stabs of concern for Pops's wellbeing since Grandma Abby died. She thought this must be what it felt like to worry about a child—or at least the closest she'd ever get. *Better than being a crazy cat lady,* she thought.

Pops changed the subject. "You're coming to the house Thursday?" It was less a question than a confirmation. They had breakfast every Sunday and dinner every Thursday, which just about summed up both of their social lives, since Rita could hardly call her occasional assignations with a married man social.

"Wouldn't miss it," she said.

Pops motioned to their waitress to bring a container for his leftovers.

"Do you have plans for the rest of the day?" Rita asked him.

I'm meeting Stan at the Veteran's Museum. He'll be there after the eight o'clock mass lets out."

"What's happening at the museum?"

"I don't know. He's volunteering for another program. He got us free tickets, I guess."

Rita smiled and shook her head. "I wonder if they know how lucky they are to have Uncle Stan. For as often as he volunteers there, he should get ten free tickets."

Stan was really Pops's nephew, making him Rita's second cousin, or once removed maybe, she couldn't keep it straight. She just always called him Uncle Stan.

"Well, It's good for him to be involved." Pops said. "With all that protesting back then. I think this makes him feel better about what went on over there."

Rita's phone chirped and vibrated on the table. She picked it up to read the text. "Oh cripes! Pops, I gotta run. There's a story breaking." She was out of the booth, shoving her phone into her bag and fishing for her keys at the same time. "I'll call you later. Tell Uncle Stan I said hi."

Outside the gusts were still blowing across the open lot. The restaurant had a huge flag out front, thrashing and clanging its rigging against the hollow metal pole that hoisted it high into the wind. She charged forward across the pavement, listening to the flutter of fabric and the sharp ringing and, every sixth beat or so, a loud crack from all that stiff cotton catching a backlash.

In the time it took Rita to get to her car, two black and whites sped past the parking lot with lights flashing and sirens blaring. Others sounded in the distance, all coming from different directions.

The wind buffeted her while she fished her car keys out of her pocket. She hit the wrong button and the bug's horn beeped. "Damn it!" Locking the car doors, no matter where, no matter what time of day, had been part of Pops's driver's training. Whatever other dangers might befall Rita, she was never going to die at the hands of a maniac lurking in her backseat.

She wasn't sure which irritated her more, Pops's hyper vigilance or the fact that she couldn't walk away from the car left unlocked without feeling like she was disappointing him.

She pulled the door open, flung her purse onto the passenger's seat and got in. Jamming the key into the ignition, she twisted it forward. The engine had barely started when she pulled the automatic shift into reverse.

Away from her grandfather's ears, she cut loose with a string of expletives, maneuvering the car out of the parking space and racing through the lot toward Marina Drive. With any luck, she'd catch the green light at the intersection with Belknap.

The Superior Police Department had been encrypting their radio communications for some time, but a text from Rita's editor said she'd picked up what sounded like a search and rescue effort on the Douglas County emergency band. Something big was happening at the Nemadji Bridge on 58th Street. Gold Cross and the Superior Fire Department EMTs were both responding.

Rita hit her steering wheel repeatedly, lobbing a few more f-bombs. She'd seen the Facebook chatter just after midnight last night. A fifteen-year-old boy had gone missing and police were combing the city looking for him. Of course the night owls in the many Superior group pages were spinning their brand of drama. It wouldn't have haunted Rita long into the night except for that one beleaguering fact–he was last seen outside the rectory of Immaculate Heart Cathedral. Having filed the story on the anniversary of the cold case a few days earlier, Rita couldn't help comparing the similarities of this disappearance to that of the Baker boy.

"Rein it in, Rita," she scolded herself. "This could be anything–could be nothing." She pushed the gas pedal closer to the floor, trying to keep up with the speeding emergency vehicles. They would blast through any red signals on East Second Street, then turn up 39th Avenue East traveling along the taconite facility rail yards. It probably would've been faster to take Stinson Avenue, the old road leading to the refinery. That was the shorter way to Bardon and with no traffic lights, but she didn't want to chance being stopped by a train.

Being the first reporter on the scene would be a coup, even if the *Telegram* didn't publish again until Tuesday. She'd be able to get the initial thoughts from the emergency crews before they had time to prepare more considered responses. She might not be able to beat the *Duluth News Tribune* to print, or scoop the local on-air news, but she could probably mine a few insights they would miss.

III

Rita turned the corner from 42nd Avenue East toward the Nemadji River. Two patrol cars blocked the road on either side of the short bridge spanning the muddy water. A uniform stood post at each approach. She slowed her bug, coming to a stop just behind the black and white cruiser. She watched the officer on guard walk toward her, admiring the precise crease of his regulation dark trousers, the well-fit button-down shirt and the wide, flat cap worn low on his brow. Police, fire, military, it didn't matter much to Rita; a man in uniform rattled her cage.

He motioned for her to roll down her window. "You'll have to turn around, ma'am."

Rita didn't recognize him. *Must be a rookie,* she thought. "What's going on?" she asked.

"I'm not at liberty to tell you that, ma'am. If you could, please, just turn your vehicle around and find another route to your destination."

His short clipped hair under the police issue cap, his rigid posture and the formal way he addressed her all added up to military service—not long off deployment. She backed her car slowly, angling toward the shoulder like she was making a Y-turn, but instead she kept backing into the graveled pull-out that provided parking for river anglers. She popped open the glove compartment and pulled out her press card, dangling from a long lanyard.

The uniform walked over to her car. "Ma'am, I'm sorry. I'd appreciate if you could continue about your business."

"Relax. I'm with the press." She flashed her I.D. out the window. "What's the story?"

He looked around with a bemused expression, likely hoping for somebody with the right answer to come rescue him.

Rita got out of her car. It was warmer away from the lake, especially in the forested gully of the riverbed where tall trees blocked the wind off its cold waters. She could smell wild valerian on the breeze, a sweet fragrance that reminded her of the centers of chocolate covered cherries. A year ago she didn't know what it was—she couldn't say if she'd ever even seen its delicate, white-pink flowers or smelled its heady scent.

Then she'd covered a story on an herbal farm and community apothecary just outside the city limits. Was it an invasive species, she asked. "Some would say so," was the reply, "but the earth provides an abundance of what we need to heal society when we need it. Valerian is a natural calmative; it alleviates anxiety and soothes wounded psyches."

Rita was skeptical, but since that day she noticed waves of its sweet flowers growing in every open field and all along the roadways. She started smelling it on the air, too, like she was now.

Reality intruded again: The medical examiner's wagon was parked on the opposite end of the bridge. That meant a dead body. Rita wasn't quite bold enough to walk past the officer and onto the bridge. She rose up on her tiptoes and craned her neck to see over his shoulder and down the embankment to the river.

There were half a dozen or more men in the water—EMTs from the fire department, along with more uniforms. The current was flowing faster than usual from the heavy rain that had fallen the week before, and the men struggled to keep their footing on the rock-strewn river bed.

"Ma'am. I don't think you should be here," the rookie said.

"Public property." Rita stood her ground." I'm not breaking the law as long as I don't cross your line. By the way, you might want to put up some yellow tape. This much excitement is going to find its way to the social media buzz pretty fast. The gawkers will descend like a swarm of mosquitoes," she said. "Thirsty for blood."

He turned his head and spoke into his radio. "Captain. I've got a reporter here. What do you want me to do with her?"

"Who is it?" The voice crackled back over the radio.

"Rita Sullivan," she called out toward the ravine. "Telegram."

"Tell her to keep her pencil in her pocket until I get up there," the voice came back over the radio.

"He said—"

"I got it. But you'd better figure this one out quick, rookie." She nodded toward the first car turning onto the road.

Across the way, an unmarked Chevy Impala drove up to the bridge. She knew the car and the detective getting out of it, Richard Drake, Rick to those who knew him well. He'd joined the force about the same time Rita started as a cub reporter with the *Telegram*. Since then, he'd worked his way up the ranks from patrol cop to desk sergeant and then detective.

Rita raised her hand to get his attention. She watched while he talked to the uniform stationed there. He started across the bridge, stopping midway. He motioned Rita to meet him, and nodded his okay at the rookie to let her pass. *Smart move,* she thought. Nobody but the handful of uniforms on the bridge would overhear their conversation.

"Rick, what the hell is happening?" She asked as soon as she reached him. "Is this the missing kid?"

He stood close and spoke quietly. "I won't know that until the body is positively identified, and even if I did, you know I can't tell you."

"So what can you give me for the paper?"

"You're asking for an official statement, right?"

"Of course. What else would I mean?"

"The call came in at 8:23. A woman out for her morning jog saw what she thought looked like a body and called 9-1-1. We don't know the identity of the victim. He appears to have drowned. There were no vehicles involved and we won't know if it was accidental or not until further investigation."

"Approximate age?"

"Not known at this time." Rick said.

"Could alcohol have been a factor?"

"We won't know that until we have the medical examiner's report, but it doesn't seem to be the case, according to my officers."

Rita looked up from her note pad. The Northland News Center team had arrived but was being held back. The videographer was setting up a shot with a view of the ravine and the embankment where the action was taking place.

"Off the record, Rick. Is it the missing boy?"

"I told you. I don't know that."

"What's your gut tell you?

"Look, Rita, there's a mom out there worrying about her son. We don't know if this is him or not, but she sure as hell doesn't need to see it plastered all over the Internet that we found a floater in the river."

"A mother, no dad?"

"If, and I said *if* it's the missing kid, his dad is on the road–drives an 18-wheeler."

Rita looked around at the clusters of cops, some standing by parked patrol cars, others on the embankment, a few scattered along the bridge either looking over the rail or standing with their backs to the water, watching the arrival of onlookers.

The curious had been dribbling in since she arrived, some walking from cars they left parked along the road in both directions, others driving their rented golf carts from the nearby course along the shoulder.

A few even wandered over from their McMansions to stand on the crest of the hill overlooking the river, though Rita could have identified them even without the geographical hint, by the cut of their crisp cotton walking shorts and slacks, genderless colors of white, khaki and navy topped with little-logo polo shirts. It was the shirts that separated them; the ladies seemed to prefer soft pastels and the men went for brighter, primary hues.

"Where's the woman who spotted the body?" Rita asked. "If she was jogging out here, she must live in one of those river mansions."

"Relax, we put her in a patrol car and took her home."

"So it's a homicide." Rick's presence on the scene pretty much confirmed it, but Rita was fishing for confirmation. After a moment of silence, she looked up from her note pad. She had to tilt her head to look at Rick's face—a good six inches above hers. His stern expression when he was working a case always took her by surprise. In the bright morning sun, she noted the deepening wrinkles at the corners of his eyes and the gray just beginning to streak through his dark brown hair.

"No comment," he said. He smiled, and his upper lip curved into his trim mustache, and the cheeks of his broad, square face rounded up and out. His smile changed his whole face, making him look somewhat goofy with his already smallish eyes narrowing to slits above the protruding cheeks.

Other than the mustache he was clean-shaven, at this time of the morning anyway. She'd seen him often enough at the end of a long shift, when the stubble of his beard cast a heavy shadow across his chin and up the sides of his face. The kind of stubble that left kiss-and-tell whisker burns.

"You're not giving me much, Rick."

"You know the drill. The department will release an official statement for the press. You'll have to wait until then."

She shoved her notebook back in her purse. "Come on, Rick, tell me what you really think. Is it the missing kid or not?" They'd been doing this dance long enough to respect each other's professional boundaries. Rita had never betrayed Rick's confidences by leaking a story before he gave her the all clear. In return, her number was on his speed dial.

"I really don't know, Rita. It could be somebody from one of the houses on the river, a domestic dispute gone too far, a kid with a snoot full from his parent's liquor cabinet. Off the record, it's probably the missing boy."

"Is that what you're going to tell *them*?" She shifted her eyes in the direction of the news teams, one from each of the local stations now, waiting up on the road, held back by the yellow tape now barricading the bridge.

His laugh was low and round, rolling up out of his barrel chest. "You never give up, do you?"

"So quit stonewalling me. You know as well as I do this is practically the anniversary of the Baker boy's murder." She whispered, keeping one eye on the news teams anxious for Rick to close the distance to where they stood. "Another young boy disappears from the rectory of Immaculate Heart, then turns up dead hours later? It could be the same murderer."

"Homicide, not murder."

"Christ! You sound just like my grandfather."

"A good cop, I'm told." He spoke through his smile, his lips barely moving for the news team cameras they both knew were rolling.

"Don't worry about them," Rita said. "They'll never run footage with a rival reporter in frame."

"Maybe not, but all those cell phones pointed at us are shooting video, and for all I know, there's an app that reads lips. He put his arm lightly on her elbow and started guiding her off the bridge.

She resisted the urge to lean into him. The scent of his cologne invaded her nostrils. She took a deep, quiet breath, inhaling the citrus-spice notes. The touch of his hand on her arm suddenly sent a shiver up her spine. She deliberately fell out of step, forcing herself to concentrate.

Rick turned toward her, his back to the crowd. He spoke in a low tone. "It could be a coincidence," he said "Or a copycat; I think somebody published a full page story on the cold case just a few days ago."

Rita's heart skipped a few quick beats before starting to pound so hard and fast she could feel it in her chest. "Are you saying my story might have caused this?"

"Rita, I was teasing you."

She looked up at him quickly, and then back down. It was long enough to catch the quick flash of concern in his soft, hazel eyes. No wonder he had a reputation on the force for being a smooth interrogator. That look of compassion tempered with cool confidence could put a mass murderer at ease.

"Rita, whoever killed the Baker kid would be well past sixty years old now, or very possibly dead."

"But it's still possible," she said. They came to the end of the bridge. "Thanks, Rick. Let me know as soon as there's an official statement?"

"You know I will."

The rookie was doing a good job of holding back the news teams, but she'd bet he was still going to get an ass chewing from his boss for letting her through before he got that tape up. Poor kid, there wasn't enough big crime in a town like Superior to give a rookie cop any experience. There'd be a lot more mistakes before he learned the ropes.

Rita ducked under the tape and skirted around the other reporters. Normally, they'd exchange pleasantries, even some facts, but Rita was rattled by the idea that her story might have somehow triggered a tragedy.

"Anything worth a headline above the fold?" They asked, in her lingo. On air, it would be a lead-in.

She kept her head down, avoiding eye contact with her colleagues and the dozen or so onlookers standing in the road. "Not much to know, yet," she said staying on course for her car. She didn't want to stick around for the rest of the pony show, with other reporters jostling for a statement from an official, hoping an officer or emergency worker straggling behind might spill something.

She walked to her car, retrieving her camera from the passenger seat. It was a simple point-and-shoot, but had enough zoom to let her get a few good shots looking back across the bridge. She snapped a couple of the riverbank and the cluster of police and EMTs scattered there, but not the gurney being hauled up the embankment and loaded into the coroner's wagon.

She'd leave the morbid stuff to the networks. By the time her coverage was published on Tuesday, the more shocking images of this scene would be old news—shown morning, noon, and night on every local channel. She didn't need to provide a print copy that would twist the guts of the victim's family for years to come.

Back inside the safe boundary of her car, she took a moment to scan the crowd. There were no houses down here other than those fronting the river along the west bank. Across 42nd Avenue East lay the rail yard, surrounded by shrubby woodland. The onlookers had followed the emergency vehicles here, anticipating a tragedy, even a bloody scene, anxious to satisfy their gruesome curiosity.

Like I'm any better, She thought. *Or maybe I'm worse; I do this for a living.*

She studied the faces she could see, looking for one that seemed more interested or excited than curious. If somebody dumped a body in the river, that somebody could be standing there now, watching. What were the odds the same person could be Thomas Baker's murderer?

She laughed at her thoughts. There's a murderer standing here, and he not only killed whoever is lying in the water, he killed the Baker kid fifty years ago. "And my story flushed him out? Get a grip, girl," she said to herself. If by some chance Thomas Baker's murderer was still alive, why would he resurface now, after getting away with it for fifty years?

She started her bug and pulled onto the roadway, heading away from the river and the grief storm brewing there. Now that she thought about it, the valerian down by that roadside smelled a lot more like funeral parlor lilies than candied cherries.

IV

It was a short five-minute drive from the river to Immaculate Heart Cathedral on the east end of town. Rita circled the block around the church and rectory, two buildings connected by a short glass and steel breezeway resembling a Victorian conservatory. The church, a brick structure over sandstone foundation, was a stunning example of Romanesque revival, if you liked that sort of thing—all arches and spires. The tallest peak housed a belfry topped with a steeple-pitched roof and a simple metal cross at its pinnacle. The mid-morning sun formed a perfect nimbus around the icon. The rectory was a smaller version, minus the steeple and cross.

It hadn't occurred to Rita that the church parking lot would be filled, but it *was* Sunday, after all, and ten o'clock mass was about to start. She drove along the rows of parked cars to find an empty space to fit the bug in, far from the building's main entrance. She killed the engine, silencing the radio just as her favorite Sunday Morning show, *A Way With Words,* was coming on air over KUWS.

Rita leaned forward, ducking to look out the windshield for a fuller view of the church and rectory. A few late stragglers were hurrying up the front steps. It was all so familiar to her, yet much less compelling now that she wasn't a child anymore. She wondered why the thought of going inside twisted her gut. She checked the sky for any signs of impending lighting bolts before leaning back into the bug's contoured bucket seat, letting the sun and the brown vinyl warm her through her thin sweater and the cotton shirt she wore beneath it.

She studied the lot and churchyard. It was the last place Thomas Baker had been seen fifty years ago, before his body was found less than two miles away, lying in a ditch along a remote stretch of Stinson Avenue.

No, that's not right. Rita reminded herself he was never actually seen at the church. Baker was one of the two altar boys scheduled to serve at the early mass, but he never showed up. It was his skateboard that placed him at the church, off to the side of the wide, tiered concrete steps, discovered in plain sight, but not until after the priest called his home to ask why he hadn't shown up for mass.

The skateboard may as well have been invisible to the rank and file parading into the church that morning, but after the news of Thomas Baker's death broke later in the evening, nearly every parishioner attending mass at Immaculate Heart that day suddenly remembered seeing the abandoned board by the steps and thinking it was odd.

Rita wondered what his parents' first thoughts might have been when the priest called their home. Did they think he was playing hooky from church? Did they suspect he'd run away? Was there a reason to think he might? When the police told them there was a body to identify, did the Bakers clutch hands going into the morgue, hoping against hope it wasn't their son? They would have known, though; deep down, they'd have had to know.

It's not like boys going missing and their bodies turning up in ditches is an everyday occurrence in Superior, Rita thought.

From deep within the recesses of her purse, Rita's phone chirped out another notice of a text message. That was one good thing about not being able to quickly retrieve her phone or anything else from the black hole at the bottom of her purse: She was never tempted to answer a call or retrieve a text while driving. She finally excavated the phone and opened the message:

> `Missing boy's mother en route to ID body.`

That was it, then. That poor woman was this very minute hanging onto the same futile hope Thomas Baker's parents had clung to fifty years ago. She was sitting at home, willing her son to be alive, praying that the body fished out of the muck in the Nemadji River wasn't *her* son. Somewhere, her husband was driving his rig with nothing left on his mind but getting home to help search for his son. If it turned out he was too late, he'd feel like that loaded truck had run him over and left him for dead. In the days to come, he'd probably wish it had.

She pulled up the paper's website and started keying in her report. She disliked typing on the small keyboard of her phone's screen, but it was a short post and she'd left her laptop at home.

> **Breaking News:** Superior police and emergency crews have responded to a report of an apparent drowning at the site of Nemadji River bridge near 58th Street and 42nd Avenue East, southeast of the golf course. Detective Richard Drake of the Superior Police Department said the identity of the victim is unknown at this time. There appeared to be no vehicles involved in the incident.

She stared at the words she'd written, feeling an uncomfortable sense of déjà vu. She knew the facts of the cold case well, and this new one felt too familiar for comfort. She posted the status on the *Telegram* website. It wouldn't be long before somebody shared it on Facebook. Then she'd be able to see if anybody else connected it to the Baker case.

She told herself there was still a chance this could turn out to be nothing more than an accidental drowning—a kid fishing on Sunday morning or a teenager who wandered away from a drinking party Saturday night.

Yeah, keep telling yourself that.

She switched her phone to silent and dropped it into her purse.

In 1966, there were four priests in residence at the Immaculate Heart rectory. There was probably only one there now. Or maybe not. With most of the churches giving up their rectories, those that still maintained residences were likely at full capacity, even if the priests served other parishes.

Who cares? Stay focused.

That was the problem with her journalist's mind—a serious case of trivia-triggered ADD. It sucked her down one rabbit hole after another until she was miles away from any point of entry.

St. Mary's Cathedral of the Immaculate Heart was the largest of Superior's Catholic churches. The name was always shortened to one of two choices—whichever one a person used was a sure tell whether or not they were Catholic. The Catholics all called it Immaculate Heart or even The Heart, while everybody else knew it simply as the Cathedral. Poor St. Mary got lost in the patriarchal scheme of things. Funny, since it was founded by an order of teaching nuns devoted to Mariology. Of course, you'd only know that if you went to school at Immaculate Heart; the story was part of the history curriculum.

So what was last night's missing boy doing at the rectory? Who'd seen him? Or was it like the Thomas Baker case—nobody had actually seen him there at all? And what time was it when he died? Could he have been going to confession? Did people still do that?

The parish included a cluster of four stone and brick buildings built late in the nineteenth century when Superior was a burgeoning city of industry. The church and rectory were on one corner, at 26th Avenue East, the school was across East 12th Street, and the convent was kitty-corner from the church. They all seemed so much smaller now than when Rita was a child.

The rectory, a place that once commanded a level of reverence just below that of the church, yet several rungs above the convent or school, was now a simple residence to her, no different than any other.

The priests who had lived there when she was a student at the Heart turned out to be the biggest letdown of all. As a child, they had seemed magical to her, holy men of God dressed in vestments of robes and stoles, presiding over mass and transforming the sacraments. Without them, there would be no need for a church. Without a church, there would be no convent or school. It was so disappointing to grow up and realize they were just human after all, some of them barely so.

In retrospect, it seemed the only fundamental pillar of Rita's parochial training that wasn't a distortion of smoke and mirrors was the nuns. Their influence never left her. But in the perfect irony that was the patriarchy, the nuns were the most overlooked—the nearly invisible handmaids vowed to a quiet life of servitude.

They were all gone now. The school and convent they'd founded even before there'd been a parish or a single priest, closed almost twenty years ago. The buildings were converted into senior residence apartments. Uncle Stan lived in one of them. Once, she asked him what it was like living in a building he'd gone to school in as a kid, but it turned out Uncle Stan hadn't gone to Immaculate Heart. He went to McCaskill on the university campus.

Stan was the only child of Pops's sister Sophie and her husband. He was a late-in-life baby, never expected but joyously welcomed, close to the same age as Rita's father. To listen to Pops, his doting mother had spoiled Stan to high heaven. Maybe that was why Rita had a soft spot for him. As an only child she bore the unfair stereotype of a spoiled brat getting lavished with attention, too. It was even worse in her case, being raised by grandparents.

Enrollment at McCaskill was by invitation only and mostly reserved for relatives of staff, or students in the Teacher Ed department who earned their practicum teaching there. Pops had enrolled at the university after returning from Korea, carrying full credits in the department. That gave Stan all he needed to get in, at least according to Sophie, who hounded Pops until he secured the invitation for her son. Sophie's husband, a Lutheran, was happy to be relieved of paying twelve years of Immaculate Heart tuition.

Uncle Stan's own recollection of how his admission had gone was a bit different. He got into McCaskill solely on his own merit, one of the best and brightest sought out by the school. That, Pops said, was a matter of opinion—mainly his sister's. But he couldn't blame her for trying to bolster her son with incessant assurances of his brilliance. Poor Stan got teased all the time because of his facial tic. He needed all the boosting he could get.

Maybe he'd have been better off at Immaculate Heart after all, Rita thought, recalling her days there. The nuns certainly didn't tolerate any kind of bullying.

Her gaze shifted to the rectory. She'd been inside the residence annexed to the back of the church only a few times, when she and Mark had attended Catholic marriage education. Marriage in the church was expected of Rita, even though she'd stopped going to mass years before and Mark wasn't Catholic.

The idea of a civil ceremony had been so far off Rita's radar it had never occurred to her. Even if it had, she wouldn't have pursued it. Rita's white-dress, big-church, tiered-cake wedding had made Grandma Abby happy. In a way, it was a blessing Grandma hadn't lived long enough to see the divorce.

Or maybe her death finally gave me the space to leave.

Rita took several sips of her lukewarm coffee, trying to wash down the resentment that rose like bile in her throat whenever she thought about her failed marriage and the church. *If I hadn't married Mark in the church, I wouldn't have had to worry about getting an annulment.* What a joke. When she found out she had grounds for an annulment, but not the money to pay for it, Rita told the pompous pricks at the diocese office what they could do with their rules.

The only thing an annulment would've given her was the infallible attestation of the *Holy Roman Catholic Church* that the fault in their marriage was not hers, proof that it had been doomed from the start and there was no saving it. It was just her selfish desire to be blameless. But, the truth was, she'd played her part in the demise of her union with Mark and she'd been doing real-life and wholly deserved penance for it ever since, more than any priest could have doled out.

Rita picked up her phone, turned it to silent and dropped it into her purse. Mass should be about half over. She swallowed the last of her coffee, wishing it were something stronger, bracing herself for what she was about to do.

Outside the car, the wind was still kicking up a fuss. Rita hurried along the length of the lot and up the front steps of the church. Inside the vestibule, she paused in front of the next set of double doors—heavy oak with thick, raised panels framed in intricate carvings. She reached for the long brass handle, darkened with age and the sweat from thousands of palms. She pulled the right-hand door open as quietly as possible.

A few heads in the back pews turned to look at her, some of the faces scowling. She'd chosen the worst possible moment to disturb their worship—the priest was raising the chalice, declaring the blood of Christ.

Rita automatically dipped her hand into the holy water font positioned in the middle of the center aisle approach, genuflecting as she made the sign of the cross. Her eyes went directly to the small shiny brass plate on the Italian marble pedestal. She already knew what it said: *In Memory of Thomas M. Baker.*

Almost as soon as Thomas's body had been found, the congregation started a reward fund for information that would lead to solving the case. The fund grew to several thousand dollars, but was never collected. It sat in an account, accruing interest for five years before the church council voted to use the money to purchase a memorial.

When the decision was announced, an anonymous donor contributed an additional $1,000 to meet the shortfall for the deluxe model, with the white alabaster bowl and two small cherubs gilded with 24-karat gold.

The font held iconic status among the youth of the parish, a touchstone to the urban legend that had grown beyond all fact over the years. They whispered the story sitting in pews, repeated it in the dark, and at one point during a more innocent time, used it to seal oaths: Swear to God on the grave of Thomas Baker? Swearing on the grave of a kid snatched off of holy ground before the sun came up, later to be found in a ditch not more than a mile away, with all the blood drained from his body, was serious business.

Rita was never sure where the idea of exsanguination originated in the first place, or if there was any truth to it. She'd tried, more than once to make connections that might lead to a clue in the case. Jesus turning water into wine, priests turning wine into blood, blood sacrifice and blood money—the anonymous donation, a possible hope for redemption? She could never make the dots connect.

The air inside the church was cool and damp. It smelled like beeswax and incense. Rita tiptoed behind the last pew on the left and then scooted around the end to slide onto the contoured wooden bench. The padded kneeler was down, for those still led by their faith to kneel for the consecration. Most, but not all, were in the reverent position. Rita remained seated, wondering if she'd missed the handshake of peace, or if it was still to come. *What is it about that handshake that I detest so much?*

Father Carmichael—she could see that's who it was now—came down from the altar to stand on the same level as the congregants. Rita thought about Grandma Abby's disappointment over the removal of the ornate communion rail, made of the same imported Italian marble as the supporting columns of the church and later the baptism font.

"I received my first communion at that rail. So did your father and your Aunt Sue," Grandma Abby had told her. "My mother told me how they worked so hard to raise the funds to pay for that rail when she was just a little girl. Such a waste."

Once communion got underway, it took less than ten minutes for those receiving the sacrament to file up to the front of the church, where the hosts and wine were being given with the help of two lay people. *Did they still call them that?*

Rita passed the time by taking in the beauty of the church's interior. Immaculate Heart didn't have the typical stone-gray cold interior of other churches. The high-domed ceilings were painted sky blue to represent the heavens, the walls were warmed with a soft blush tint, and all of the wood trim was painted with a pristine white-lacquer finish. Gold leaf adorned the raised reliefs of every cornice on the narrow pillars separating the side aisles from the center of the church. Painted gold stars were scattered across the ceiling.

The main altar was a magnificent artifact reaching a height of nearly thirty feet, all of it hand-carved and richly painted. The repetition of tiered arches rose above the altar table, forming alcoves that housed cherubs and glorious angels up to the midpoint. Just above them, Joseph and Mary reigned on either side with the crowned glory directly above them, Jesus on the cross.

According to her Aunt Sue, the priests used to serve Mass at that altar, far removed from the congregation with their backs to the pews nearly the entire time. It made no sense to Rita, but little about the church, then or now, ever did.

Immaculate Heart had two smaller altars, not nearly as ornate, located in each alcove of the cruciform, facing each other across the transept. Rita recalled placing a bouquet at the foot of the Virgin Mary's altar on her wedding day.

Joseph did not hold court on the opposite side, as one would expect. Rather, it was Mary Magdalene's altar. Rita remembered her amusement that day, walking to the Virgin's altar all regaled in white lace, wondering what the church full of guests would think if she offered her floral homage to Magdalene instead, the whore turned saint.

The communicants filed back into the pews, bowing their heads in silent prayer. Rita sat there wondering when she'd become a heretic. She had loved the beauty of Immaculate Heart when she was a child, the pomp and circumstance of the vestments, the mystery of the liturgy, the candles and incense, bells and chanting. All of it had been so magical to her.

The conclusion of the service didn't take long. Rita found herself just as anxious as she'd been as a school child to hear the parting words of the priest, "The mass had ended, go in peace."

"Thanks be to God," She responded with the congregation, translating her personal interpretation in her head: *Thank God mass is over. Now I can leave.*

Rita had no particular beef against the Catholic religion, or any religion for that matter. Her childhood wasn't filled with the horror stories of parochial school uniforms, knuckles smacked with rulers, kneeling on dried peas, or other absurdities she'd heard. She hadn't been required to attend mass every morning before classes began, like her father and Aunt Sue had, before the Vatican II reforms. She'd never had a nun put a Kleenex on her head because she'd forgotten a chapel veil. Rita simply had no interest in conforming to the archaic dogma of organized religion.

She stayed in her pew at the back of the church until all but a few of the worshippers had made their way outside the building. Then she stood and took her place in the recession, bringing up the rear. She couldn't recall the priests standing in the vestibule when she was a child, glad-handing the parishioners as they exited the way Father Carmichael was doing now. Maybe that because she'd always ducked out right after communion. This was working in her favor, though. Today she wanted to talk to Father Carmichael.

He stood just beyond the open doors to the vestibule reaching for her hand as she approached. "God bless you this morning." He looked closely at her face while shaking her hand. "Are you a guest of our church?"

"Not exactly." Rita wasn't surprised he didn't remember her. He'd seen her exactly two times since she left Immaculate Heart School, at her wedding and at Grandma Abigail's funeral. Brides and mourners probably all tend to run together after the first thousand or so. "I attended school here when I was a child, before it closed. Oh, and church, of course," she said.

"You do look a bit familiar. Are you visiting home then?"

"No, I live in Superior. Always have."

"Well, whatever brings you here today, I'm pleased to see you, Miss—"

"Sullivan. Rita Sullivan."

"Oh my goodness, yes. I remember you. Dave and Abigail's granddaughter." His face clouded. "Is your grandfather well?"

"Pops is fine. I'm fine. We're all good."

He relaxed. "Oh, I'm glad to hear that. I don't see much of him since your grandmother passed."

A short, but awkward silence followed. Rita waited for Father Carmichael to fill it.

"Is there something you need, Rita?"

"I wanted to talk to you, Father. In private if that's possible."

"Certainly. I could give you a few minutes now, or do you need more time? I can meet you in the rectory and set an appointment on the calendar if you do."

"I wanted to ask you about the young boy who went missing from here last night."

Deep furrows appeared across his forehead. He tilted his chin up a bit while he searched his memory, then his eyes registered a deeper comprehension.

"I'm afraid," he said, "that I cannot comment for the press."

V

"Now, if you'll excuse me," Father Carmichael said, trying to pass. He'd connected her name with her byline in the paper, not a difficult feat considering there were only two reporters on staff. Normally Rita appreciated the recognition, unless people fawned; pandering made her uneasy. On the other hand her notoriety could be annoying when it caused people to clam up, like this.

"I'm not inquiring for the paper, Father. A body was found in the Nemadji River this morning, and I can't help wondering what you might know about that."

"A boy? Found in the river?"

So much for not commenting. "Yes."

"I can't discuss this with you."

"Can't or won't?" Rita asked.

His left eyebrow went up a little. "I'm beginning to remember you now, Rita. You always wanted all the answers—no loose ends. I suppose that's what makes you such a good reporter. As I recall it didn't bode well for the quality of your faith."

Rita laughed. His shaming tactic resurrected an old ghost from her past. "T.D.T.D," she said. "All the best Catholics, right?"

"Too dumb to doubt?" he asked. "Still wielding that sword, are you?"

"I deal in facts," Rita said. "Not fairy tales. The church prefers followers who don't question."

"Tell me, if you're not inquiring for the paper, what is it then? Idle curiosity?"

"You might say that."

"I'd be happy to explore this further when we both have sufficient time, but if what you're telling me is true, I have to contact the boy's mother."

"You won't reach her now. She's with the police." Rita decided to try a new line of attack. "Father Carmichael, are you aware of the significance in the timing here?"

"I'm afraid I don't follow you."

Rita turned and pointed to the holy water font behind them.

"Thomas Baker." The priest's voice registered just above a whisper. The slump of his shoulders told Rita he knew exactly what she was inferring.

"Don't you think it's an odd coincidence, Father, that another boy has disappeared from this church and turned up dead?" Rita was fully aware of the fact that she had no proof the body they'd fished out of the river was the missing boy. *Forgive me if I'm lying to a priest.*

"Ms. Sullivan—is that right, or do you prefer Miss?" he asked. "I'm sorry. I never know the proper title in these situations, when a woman sloughs off her married name after a divorce."

Nice dig. Screw the remorse for lying; the gloves are off, Rita thought. "Whatever you're comfortable with, Father," she said.

"Thank you. Then, you'll please excuse me, because this entire conversation is making me uncomfortable."

"Why is that, Father?"

"According to you, a family in my parish is in the midst of personal tragedy. Their need is of greater concern to me at this point than providing you with a good quote for your paper. Neglecting that duty causes me discomfort. And since I can only assume the police are already mounting an investigation, the thought that I might be handing over pertinent facts to the press also makes me very uncomfortable—despite your assurance that this isn't for the paper."

He tried to walk past her again but Rita took a step in front of him. "Just one more question, Father. In 1967, a priest from this parish, Father Bartoelli, left very suddenly and with little explanation. Was he abusing young boys? Is that why he was sent away?" Two other priests from the same time in the church's history had been suddenly reassigned to new parishes. They'd since been accused of molestation.

"Miss Sullivan. I was not here in 1967. I was not even out of high school. I have no idea of the circumstances surrounding this Father Bartoelli's departure. Now, if you'll excuse me." Father Carmichael didn't wait for her leave. He brushed past her and retreated up the aisle.

Rita watched him hurry away. He stopped for a quick genuflection and sign of the cross at the foot of the chancel. Then he turned and disappeared into the only part of the church that still remained a mystery to Rita, the sacristy. It had long been rumored there was a tunnel leading from that private chamber to the rectory basement, allowing the priests to come and go undetected. For what nefarious deeds, she could only imagine.

She stood there in the doorway looking down the length of the nave with its rows and rows of pews, the altar and the statues, the decorative painting, soft lighting casting a warm glow over all of it. She missed the sense of wonderment she'd once felt there, the majesty of space and the comfort of familiar ceremony.

It was Grandma Abby and Pops who had brought Rita to church every Sunday after her father died, to the occasional Christmas and Easter service before that. The first time she asked Aunt Sue why her father didn't go to church, she was told he just stopped believing. The story changed when she grew older and Aunt Sue thought the truth wouldn't be as harsh.

Rita stepped back into the church, feeling more at ease now that it was empty. She walked to the Virgin Mary's altar, tucked into the alcove to the left of the pews. She was delighted to see the stand of devotional candles still in place, with rows of cobalt blue votive glasses, some glowing from the candles lit within.

She took her wallet out of her purse, found a five dollar bill to drop into the donation box, and then lit three candles—one for Thomas Baker, one for Sean Nolan and one for her father, Francis—Frankie—Sullivan.

Rita heard a door open and close from the depths of the sacristy, the click of the latch resounding like the last note played on the pipe organ in the balcony, slowly fading to silence. She always admired the acoustic quality of an old church and often thought it a waste that Immaculate Heart didn't have an active choir. The chance to lift her voice in song might be enough to bring her back to the flock. Rita was sure the popularity of karaoke bars directly correlated to the demise of active church choirs—people just wanted a place to sing.

Rita didn't immediately recognize the priest emerging from the shadowed archway. He walked toward the center aisle without looking up, unaware of her presence. It was something in his stride that looked familiar, though, like somebody she knew.

"Jim?"

He looked up at the sound of his name. She saw his face light with recognition.

"Rita?"

Jim and her father had been best friends, not that she actually remembered that, but she did recall his visits when she was growing up, dropping by now and then to see Pops and Grandma Abby. He always brought some small gift for Rita, and he called her Gila. It was the nickname her father had given her. Aunt Sue said it was because she'd been born almost two weeks late, all wrinkled and blotchy, with scaly dry patches on her skin. Her father said she'd looked like a shriveled lizard and, from that moment, started calling her his little Gila monster.

Jim's visits dwindled as Rita got older. He came around a few times when she was a teenager, but the length between appearances kept getting longer each time until it stretched into years, and then stopped all together. She'd thought about him once in a while and wondered where he'd gone and what he was doing. And then, out of the blue, he showed up at Grandma Abby's funeral eight years ago—in a priest's frock no less.

"Rita, what brings you here?" he asked.

"I'm not really sure."

He chuckled. "I'd be careful of that. I'm still not sure how I ended up a priest. I know there was a lot of drugs and lost years, and then one morning I woke up wearing this collar."

Rita smiled. "You are so full of it. I'm still not buying that story no matter how many times you tell it."

"It's mostly true. The drugs and lost years anyway, but we covered all that at your grandmother's funeral." He reached out and took both of her hands. "Gila, you know, I still feel bad that I wasn't there for you when you were growing up."

"You? Why?"

"Let's sit." He guided her to the nearest pew, standing aside to let her in first. When she sat down, he slid in next to her. "Rita, your dad was the best friend I ever had—like a brother. I introduced him to your mother, you know. Though, I never thought he'd marry her."

"He had to. Knocked her up I hear."

Jim laughed. "Frankie never did anything he didn't want to do; that I can say without a doubt. He loved your mother, *really* loved her, and you too."

"So I've been told." She changed the subject. "I didn't know you were in Superior. Are you visiting?"

"No. I've been assigned to this parish, sort of, for now. I've been floating around for a few years, filling in at any of the churches that need an extra hand. Father Carmichael is having some surgery soon, so I'll be taking over his duties while he recovers."

Rita knew that the polite thing to do would be to ask him whether the surgery was serious. But she was in a hurry, and really didn't give a damn about Father Carmichael's health at the moment. "When did you get here?"

"Late Friday night. I spent most of the day yesterday at the diocese office and today I'm just hanging out, getting a feel for Father Carmichael's routine. I planned to pay a visit to you and Pops as soon as I was more settled in. How's he doing, without your grandmother?"

"He's good. He still misses her an awful lot, but he's a survivor."

"I'd expect no less of Dave Sullivan."

"Jim, or should I call you Father Wiese?"

"How about Father Jim?"

"Why did you become a priest, really? I mean it's not like you had a calling; you were older. Did you ever even get married? Did you have any kids?"

"None that have claimed me. And no, I never married. But the call doesn't always come early in life, Rita. Or who knows, maybe it did and I was so strung out on drugs I didn't hear the phone ringing."

"Funny. Did you go to Immaculate Heart? Is that how you and my dad met?"

"I was a grade ahead of him in school. We got to know each other because we were altar boys together." He smiled. "Such a long time ago."

"Were those priests here, then, the ones that have been accused of sexual abuse?" She knew they were. She'd listened to her Aunt Sue's stories and speculation enough times.

Jim bowed his head down and closed his eyes.

"I guess that answers my question," she said.

He looked back up at her. "What's this about, Rita?"

"Was my father molested? My aunt thinks he was."

"Sue. Sweet Sue."

Rita thought she heard a hint of affection in his voice. Maybe he'd come around those early years because of Aunt Sue.

"Your dad and your aunt were tight," he said. "Frank was quite the protective big brother and Sue adored him. I think it broke her heart when he got into the drugs. It took him away from her."

"She said she remembered a time my dad went to camp, something connected with the church. She said he called home sobbing, begging Pops and Grandma to come get him and take him home."

Jim shook his head. "I don't remember any church camps. That's more an evangelical thing than Catholic. Are you sure it wasn't the Boy Scouts?"

"She said it was the church, for the altar boys. Why, was he in Scouts? Were both of you?"

"I wasn't. I'm not sure if your dad was. I mean, I know I should remember something like that, but my memory is not the best."

Rita weighed her next question before asking. "Did you know what those priests were doing?"

"Not then," Jim said. "They never would have bothered a guy like me. And the ones they did mess with weren't talking about it."

Jim was a burly man, tall and broad shouldered, built like a linebacker. Rita guessed he'd probably been one of the bigger boys in school. Her father had been a puny kid, the 98-pound weakling. It was easy for Rita to pick him out in his old class photos; he was always the smallest one.

"Not then, so you found out later. Who told you?" she asked.

"Not your dad, if that's what you're thinking. Listen, Rita, your Aunt Sue lost her brother long before he died. He started running away from home when he was fifteen. He dropped out of school halfway through his senior year."

"I know that," Rita said.

"But you don't know why, and Sue doesn't want to admit the truth. Your grandfather and your dad, they were like chlorine and ammonia, guaranteed to be caustic when they came in contact with each other."

"Sue always said Pops was a lot more strict with my dad and her than when I was growing up."

"He wasn't just strict, Rita. He used to knock your dad around pretty good."

"Pops?" Rita's heart beat faster.

"I'm not telling you this to disparage him. He's a good man. He's always been a good man in many ways. There was just some dynamic there . . ."

Rita drew in a deep breath. Her grandfather was a pillar. He was a staunch disciplinarian and he could be stubborn, but she'd never seen him lose his temper. She shook her head, as if she could rid it of the image Jim was imprinting there. "I don't believe it. I can't."

"Before your father's funeral, when the family had their last moments of private visitation at the funeral home, before they closed the casket, your grandfather asked to be left alone with your father. I was with the rest of your family, everybody waiting for Pops to come out so they could get into the limos. Your grandmother asked me to go back and get him—he was holding things up. I found him sobbing over your father's body, apologizing and begging forgiveness for being so hard on him. He kept saying if he'd only know how short their time was going to be he'd have done things differently."

Rita shifted uncomfortably in the pew. She wiped away the tears that welled up in her eyes and spilled over onto her cheeks.

"I'm sorry Rita. I wish I didn't have to tell you this. I wouldn't hurt you for the world."

"It doesn't make any sense. Pops doesn't have a mean bone in his body."

"Maybe he learned a hard lesson with your father. Besides, it was a different era. A belt, a switch cut from the lilac bush outside, a quick backhand across the face. The same thing was happening in every second house on the block back then."

"Is that why my dad started taking drugs?"

A sudden gust of wind rattled the windows of the old church. Rita shivered, but not from any draft. It felt more like her body was trying to shake off the assault being waged against her memories.

"Like I said. There were a lot of drugs to be had. We were young and fearless—immortal, we thought. Drugs were just something to do, to experience. I don't know if any of us ever had more of a reason than that."

"What about my Uncle Stan?"

"Stan?"

"My grandmother always blamed Stan. She said he was the one who got my dad on drugs in the first place, after Stan got out of the army."

Jim shook his head. "She might have believed that, but it's not true. I don't remember Stan even being around much."

"I think he started hanging around more after my dad died, sort of filling an empty spot for Pops."

"That must have been difficult for your grandmother, feeling like her husband was replacing their son. There could have been some resentment there."

"Did you know Thomas Baker?" Rita asked.

"The kid that got killed? Yeah I remember him. He was a few years younger."

"Was he *experiencing* drugs?"

"I'm not sure, maybe. Why?"

"I don't know. He went to church here, he disappeared from here. He was a *little guy,* the kind the priests like to molest."

"That's harsh," Father Jim said.

"Most truths are."

"Rita, I can't give you the answers you're looking for. Your father never said a word to me about any priest molesting him, or even trying to. I have no idea about the Baker boy. Given the time frame, I suppose it's possible, but do I think any priest would have gone so far as to commit murder? That's a bit of a stretch."

"Did you know Father Bartoelli?"

"Yes. He was a priest here, all the altar boys served mass with him."

"Why did he leave?"

"Don't know, but he's never been accused of abusing anybody, like the others."

"Do you know where he is now?"

"Not a clue. I don't know if he's even still alive. It's been a long time, Rita."

"Fifty years. Thomas Baker disappeared from this church fifty years ago this Sunday. And now, last night, another young boy went missing. They fished his body out of the Nemadji River earlier this morning."

"Sean?"

Rita was surprised. "You know too?"

"The police were at the rectory last night," he said.

"Why is it nobody seems to think this is more than an odd coincidence? Was he an altar boy here? Why was he at the church on a Saturday evening?"

"I think you're grasping at straws, Rita. First you tell me you suspect Father Bartoelli may have been molesting boys, even your father. You think he might have had something to do with the Baker boy's death—and you're connecting that with the missing boy now? Father Bartoelli isn't here, hasn't been here for decades. What sense does that make?"

"I don't know. None, I guess. I just know that my father hated this church—didn't want my grandparents to take me here when he was still alive, Aunt Sue told me that much. I know he abused drugs, ran away all the time, dropped out of school. All those things are recognized signs of abuse now."

She stood up. She wanted out of the pew, but Father Jim wasn't moving aside. She contemplated climbing over the back of the wooden bench to escape.

"I thought it made perfect sense, that a priest or priests molested my father," she said. "Then you tell me my grandfather was beating my dad, even though he's never laid a hand on me or anybody else I know of. You're right; none of it makes any sense."

"I didn't exactly say *beating*."

"Well, that's what you meant."

"Look, Rita, I know it's was a lousy break, being raised without your father—or mother. You're trying to make sense of it, you're hoping for answers that might give you some peace."

"Do you think my father killed himself?"

Father Jim stood up beside her. "You're father didn't choose to abandon you, Rita. You were a precious jewel in his life. You were the reason he cleaned up his act, got a job. You were his reason for living, Rita, not for dying." He put a hand on her shoulder, briefly. "I would tell you to pray for guidance, to ask for the peace you want, but I don't think it would help you at this point."

Rita rolled her eyes. "Let me out please. I have to go."

Father Jim stepped aside and Rita blazed past him.

He called after her. "Your father was a bit of a philosopher. Did you know that?"

Rita stopped her march down the aisle. "No." She didn't turn around.

"If he could see me now, dressed like this, in this place, he'd be on his back rolling in the aisle, laughing until his gut ached." He walked toward her as he talked.

Rita smiled to herself.

"He wasn't a nonbeliever, Rita. He just didn't see God—or *a* god—in any conventional way. He thought of it more as energy for goodness, Divine energy I'd call it. And he believed it was something inside each of us, that we could nurture it or starve it but either way it was collective and as such had the power to alter the universe."

Rita turned to look at him. "But people can be good and moral, they can create peace without believing in God or following any religion."

"Of course they can. Don't tell anybody I said so, but it's all semantics. I've chosen this path and named my God. I believe that following the teachings of Jesus Christ and the Catholic Church is one way to eternal life and it's all laid out for me to follow, but I doubt it's the *only* way. What I'm trying to tell you is that you have to find *your* way Rita. You have to make your own peace."

VI

Rita's hunch was right. The body in the river was Sean Nolan's. Her story ran in the *Telegram*'s Tuesday edition.

> Police are investigating a possible homicide in Superior. The body of fifteen-year-old Sean Nolan was discovered in the Nemadji River early Sunday morning. Nolan's mother reported the boy missing shortly before midnight on Saturday, after returning home from her shift as a CNA at a local assisted-living facility.
>
> An immediate search of Nolan's neighborhood turned up the boy's bicycle, found laying on its side in the gravel beneath the East 2nd Street overpass at 27th Avenue East. Nolan's mother told police that he often used the corridor alongside the tracks to avoid crossing the busy, main thoroughfare from their home on East First Street.
>
> The roadway is accessible by motor vehicle for track crews and other utility vehicles. However, Detective Richard Drake said the absence of any damage to Nolan's bicycle indicated a vehicle had not struck the boy. He speculated that injuries sustained in a fall on the rough crushed rock of the ballast grade might have caused the boy to leave the bike and attempt walking home. In the case of a head injury, he may have been disoriented and become lost. It would be unlikely for the boy to walk the several miles from where his bicycle was located to the bridge near 42nd Avenue East and 59th Street, said Detective Drake. The police are looking for anybody who may have seen Nolan, or offered him a ride.

Rita tossed the day-old newspaper to the floor. There was more to the story, but she rarely read beyond the first few paragraphs, knowing that she'd only see the hundreds of ways she could have written it better. What mattered were the facts, and she had included them all. The medical examiner's report, the detective's speculation of possible means of death, the fact that accidental death could not be ruled out, and an exclusive statement from the Nolan family, filtered through Father Jim at Immaculate Heart.

The Nolans' statement pitched the standard cliché of a good kid from a good family, liked by everybody, above average student and Sunday school youth leader. He was a responsible boy, helped out at home, had many friends and no enemies. His family couldn't imagine anybody wanting to harm him.

Rita was sitting on her faded brown sofa with her legs curled tight to one side. She wore an oversized plain white t-shirt. Detective Richard Drake leaned back into the opposite corner of the sofa, wearing a pair of cut-off gray sweatpants.

"So basically he was an altar boy," Rita said to Rick. "Pretty much a given if you attended Immaculate Heart. He babysat the brats in Sunday school because you have to volunteer for some church duty to meet confirmation requirements, and he took out the garbage for his mom once a week."

They'd already made short work of the spring rolls, pho, and fried rice with shrimp from the New China restaurant on Belknap. Cardboard cartons, mostly empty now, cluttered the coffee table. The lingering aroma of steamed shrimp and rice, exotic spice blends, and peanut sauce was the only remaining evidence of their hedonfest. That, and their discarded clothes strewn in every room of Rita's apartment.

"Sounds about right for the average teenage boy," Rick said. He stretched his long legs stretched out to the coffee table, where he propped his feet.

Rick came from a large family, with sisters and brothers both. Rita was an only child, and never had children of her own. She figured he knew more about the rituals of young men growing into manhood than she ever would, so she was anxious to hear his take on Sean Nolan.

She leaned forward to reach for the opened wine bottle on the table, topping off two large glasses with the slightly dry pinot noir rosé recommended by the liquor store clerk. She'd wanted something to pair well with the Asian food. Rita mostly chose her wine by the look of the bottle. If the color or the shape was unique, or if the label was the least bit artsy, it was okay in her book. Rick had more discriminating tastes.

Rick took the glass Rita had poured for him. For a man pushing fifty, he still had a body worth looking at. His belly was taut, and she could see the slightest hint of a six-pack above the band of his sweatpants. His ribs broadened out from his waist up to some decent pecs—a good thing, because man boobs would have to be a deal breaker.

"The Nolan kid wasn't any different than most boys his age." Rick said.

"Come on, Rick. You were fifteen once. Fifteen-year-old boys are about as far from being perfect angels as it gets. Especially the Catholic ones, in my experience."

"Which I'm guessing was considerable," Rick said.

"Funny man. I meant observation; in my observation fifteen-year-old boys are never angels.

"Are you telling me you *never* participated in Catholic school girl shenanigans?"

"I'm telling you I'll never tell."

She enjoyed the banter and wished they had more opportunities for it, but their relationship was complicated, to say the least. Forget the fact that Rick was married. Given that he and his wife had been living separately for more than two years now, most of the community would barely blink at their affair—aside from his two teenage daughters. But a lead detective with the Superior Police Department being in bed, literally, with a member of the press would cause a scandal of epic proportion, ending both their careers.

All of this meant their passionate encounters were hit and miss—heavy on the misses. Most often they turned into a prolonged litany of food, wine, and fast sex that whetted their appetite for more of the same. After their initial passions were sated and their stamina waned, they finally indulged in the sweet dessert of more languorous lovemaking. The kind that made Rita want to cuddle up and fall asleep when it was over, arms and legs still tangled together. But that never happened.

She reached over to the coffee table, checking each wax-lined carton for any remains of the feast. She found a cold spring roll. "Want some?"

"Nope. It's all yours," Rick said.

"What would we do without the New China?" she asked.

The New China replaced the old Lan Chi's about a year earlier without warning or fanfare. It was located in one side of Superior's iconic Patio Cafe on Belknap, across from the courthouse. Judges, lawyers, laborers, working girls, and housewives had frequented the Patio. It was so well remembered in Superior that even Rita, who wasn't born until after its demise, heard tales of its renown.

In contrast, the New China was the kind of place people thought twice about going into. But once you got past its run-down exterior, the food kept you coming back. For Rick and Rita, it was all about the convenience. The New China was a half-block from the station. Rita usually called in the order, and Rick picked it up when he left the station.

They kept their relationship under wraps, making sure they were never seen together in public outside of working hours. Once quitting time came and went for the office staff, Rick could leave his personal vehicle in the municipal lot and walk the short distance to Rita's apartment. If anybody happened to see his car, they'd just assume he was working overtime. If anybody in the station had figured out where he was going, they weren't blabbing. The police protected their own, both on and off the job.

Rick was still a married man. He was married when Rita met him, very happily so. Rita was also still married, though not quite as happily. The reporter and the cop, both at the front end of their careers, Rita working the police blotter and Rick a rookie patrol cop at the bottom of the department chain of command.

It turned out he wasn't such a bad egg—and handsome in the uniform he wore before making detective. He was smart, too; that was a plus in Rita's column. But it was his unlikely mix of brawn and mercy, rare in his line of work that weakened Rita's knees.

It took some effort to keep their friendship platonic, at least on Rita's part. She couldn't say if the same was true for Rick until after the accident, when his sudden vulnerability took them both by surprise. Rita was more than happy to welcome him into the comfort of her arms, and her bed.

"Trust me," Rick said. "There's not a lot going on in a fifteen-year-old's life that would get him killed. Not in Superior."

He was right about that. There might be a disproportionate rate of poverty in their tired old industrial town, but it didn't have any inner city neighborhoods. Gang activity was pretty much non-existent. They had their share of drug traffic, but the crimes it produced were usually high-profile ones. A lot of them wound up seriously botched by the guilty parties, and that was that. LA it was not.

"Regardless," Rita said, "Sean Nolan is dead, so now his life was exemplary. I'm not saying it isn't the typical story we hear whenever a young person dies, or that it *shouldn't* be. I'm just saying it's always whitewashed. The kid had to have some flaws. His dad is never home, his mom works every afternoon. If he was like most teenagers, he slept in until noon during the summer. Not a lot of parent-child one-on-one going on in that house."

"Your point?" Rick asked.

"What was he doing every day from the time his mother left until she got back home after 11 p.m.? Where did he hang out, and who did he hang out with? Is there anything in his online history that might be questionable?"

"Like you haven't checked to see if he has Facebook or Twitter," Rick said.

"Try Snapchat and Instagram. You'd better get with the times, officer. Facebook is *so* their parents' social media. I'm talking about his search history. What was he into? Drugs? Porn?"

"I never knew you had such a dark view," Rick said.

She rolled her eyes. "What teen boy isn't looking at porn online?"

"I believe what you're trying to get out of me, is whether I've found any leads worth pursuing. The answer is yes."

"Can you tell me?"

"No."

"I'll tell you what I think," Rita said. "He wasn't doing yard work around that church to earn a little pocket change. I'm pretty sure they already pay a maintenance man to do that—and if it's more than one person can keep up with, the men's altar society would be pitching in, dragging their own kids along to help out. I can even see a kid being assigned a little yard work in the hot sun as penance for some sin. But this innocent summer job story his family is feeding you and the press, I don't believe it."

"How do you know his father isn't in the altar society? Maybe he volunteered his son for work."

Rita fixed her eyes on his, her silence saying loud and clear that she wasn't buying what he was selling.

There was a long standoff. Finally, Rick said, "Father Carmichael was doing Nolan's mom a favor. He'd been hanging out with some questionable kids and she wanted to keep him busy."

Rick sometimes broke the rules and shared facts not meant for the press with Rita. Usually some small tidbit that might have made it into a story she'd already written, but wouldn't stand alone.

"What kids?" she asked.

Rick returned his version of the silent stare.

"Okay, then. What about the parents? Are they suspects?" she asked.

"They always are, but both have airtight alibis. She was at work and the father was 500 miles away."

"How'd Sean get along with his old man? Any trouble there?"

"Some. Kids are kids," Rick said. "The boy was having growing pains. His father tried to keep him on the straight and narrow. It wasn't easy to do from the cab of his truck. Nothing new, or newsworthy, about that."

"So nobody's perfect after all. What a surprise." She took a sip of her la-de-da *pinot noir rosé*, licking its dry-tart flavor from her lips after swallowing. She preferred the Spring Creek pink Moscato from the grocery store, aisle 2E.

"It was the same way with the Baker boy," she said. "The papers were all saying what a great kid he was, and that photo they ran was positively angelic. But if you talk to any of his classmates, they'll tell you he was a real smart ass, always asking for it."

"Pubescent boys tend to be that way most of the time. Except around their mothers. Around their mothers they're sweet as pie and innocent as the day they were born. So, why are we talking about the Baker boy?"

"Oh, please. You see the similarities in the two cases same as I do. You know it's got to be the same killer."

"I *know* no such thing."

"But you're thinking about it."

"Look, Rita, this is a big case, you know that. I have to cross every *t* and dot every *i*. I have to be sure of every single fact. I don't have your luxury of jumping to the most obvious conclusion."

Rita sat up straight and set her glass down with a clink on the hard surface of her cheap Formica tabletop. She couldn't have a wood-topped table. She never knew where a coaster was when she needed it, and she spilled stuff all the time. "Don't try to change the subject by pissing me off with an insult," she said.

"What I mean is that I can't take the most obvious probability and ignore the rest of the facts."

Rita held up her index finger. "The boys were both the same age–"

"No, they weren't. Thomas Baker was 14, Sean Nolan was 15."

"Oh, please. Can you find a tinier nit to pick?" She kept the first finger up. "They were both members of Immaculate Heart, they were both altar boys, and they both disappeared from the church grounds," she said, wiggling the four fingers on her upheld hand.

"Circumstantial," Rick said. "The Baker kid was never actually seen at or near the church the morning he disappeared."

Rita kept pitching her theory. "Now that I think of it, Baker's body was found on Stinson Road, one of only two major roadways from East End to the bridge where they found Nolan. Everybody assumed Baker's killer dumped him on the road to the oil refinery because it's so remote, but it connects with Bardon, and Bardon leads right to that bridge, with absolutely nothing in between, not even a crossroad." She held up her thumb. "That's five."

"You think Baker's killer was on the way to that bridge, and something stopped him? That's quite a stretch," Rick said.

"Sean Nolan disappeared and turned up dead almost to the day of the fiftieth anniversary of Thomas Baker's murder." She held the index finger of her other hand straight up for a moment before pointing it at Rick. "And don't you dare say homicide—I'm warning you."

"I wouldn't dream of it." He pressed his lips together and crossed his arms in front of his chest.

"What?" Rita demanded.

He uncrossed his arms but hesitated for a moment before speaking. "I'm just curious, Rita. You're determined to link these two cases, but what is it about the Baker kid's death that gets you all tied up in knots? You weren't even born when it happened."

Rita let out a deep breath. "I'm not sure. I mean, everybody that ever went to Immaculate Heart knew the story, or the distorted version that grew over the years of telling, but it didn't really grab me until right after I started at the *Telegram*. I was researching a story and stumbled onto the coverage of the Baker case. I was stunned when I read that Pops was on the desk the night the call came in, when they found the body."

"I'm not following. Why would that surprise you?"

"Pops was always telling stories about his years on the force, but I'd never known he took that call, or that he was involved in the case at all." She could see Rick was still confused. "I know, two and two make four. The thing is I never had a reason to do the math before. I never knew exactly when Pops left the force—sometime in the Sixties. Until I read that article, I just assumed he left before the Baker kid was killed."

"Because he never talked about it," Rick said. "But that's not unusual for an unsolved case. Too much hearsay could jeopardize a conviction if it ever made it to court."

"I suppose. I just think it stays with him, you know? The fact that it was never solved—a murder on his watch. I've even wondered if that's why he left the department."

"I doubt that. From what I've head there'd be better reasons for a man to leave the force back then, starting with a Chief of Police that everybody believes was a little more than shady."

"What about you?"

"Do I believe the chief was a crook?"

"No. How will you feel if you never solve the Nolan case?"

"It would be tough, but I sure wouldn't quit the force over it. Besides, I have a feeling about this one. It's not going to go like the last time."

Rita leapt on his Freudian slip. "So you *do* agree. Baker and Nolan were killed by the same man, and it was murder."

Rick laughed. "Are you sure you're not Super Girl, or Wonder Woman? Because the leaps you make are astounding. I agree the cases are similar, not that both crimes were committed by the same person."

Rita was used to sparring with Rick and she thought they were equally matched, for the most part. But debating the facts in traffic cases or kibitzing over the nuance of witness statements after a case was settled in court was one thing; exchanging theories on an active homicide was altogether different. She was surprised he'd shared this much with her.

"How do you break somebody's neck?" she asked.

"And another superhuman leap." Rick said.

"The coroner's report listed cause of death as a C-2 cervical fracture from a sudden twisting motion." She pulled her legs back up onto the sofa, tucking them beneath her sitting on her heels. She leaned toward Rick, almost hovering. "A broken neck," she said. "That's what killed him."

"The same injury could have been caused by falling down the river embankment and doing a header into the water, or by the motion of the current after his head was caught in the branches of that fallen tree that snagged him and kept the body from drifting out to Lake Superior." Rick reasoned.

"As I see it, there are three scenarios," Rita said, ignoring Rick's arguments. "Both deaths were accidental, both were intentional homicides, or you have one of each."

"Amazing! You've really honed your deduction skills."

She frowned at him. "But see, there's this word *accident*. Accidents are random, right? It's unlikely two of them would have such similar circumstances. And the odds are even less that an accident and one intentional homicide would have such similar circumstances. That leaves two intentional murders."

Rick chuckled. "Okay, I'll go along with that just to hear the rest of this theory."

"If Sean's death was intentional, then somebody had to break his neck. How do you do that? Just grab and twist?"

"I know as much about it as you do—or did you think that might be part of our police training?"

"I don't know; you were a marine, right? They teach you all that stuff don't they—hand to hand combat, self defense?"

Rick shook his head. "Me? Hell no, that's Special Forces," he said. "Obviously I'm making you watch too many Steven Seagal movies. Maybe we'd better lay off of them for a while."

"Oh—please—no," Rita said each word with a deliberate monotone meant to mock him. No need for Rick to know she actually enjoyed the schmaltzy good-guys-win movies almost as much as he did. Worse, she probably liked them for the same reason he did—even if he wasn't aware of it. There was an uncanny resemblance between the young actor in those movies, and the man sitting next to her on the sofa, one that went way beyond physical appearance. Rick saw himself fighting the good fight, striking a blow for justice. He might not be taking down evil corporations, or fighting the enemy on a submerged submarine, but he knew he was one of the good guys.

VII

Rick put his feet on the floor and sat up straight, stretching his arms forward and then back. Pivoting at his waist, he did a few quick turns to both sides then took a deep breath, blowing it out audibly.

"Can we cut to the chase?" he asked. "What are you trying to get out of me?"

He was obviously losing his patience now. She was running out of time to win her point. "Pops believes the Baker boy's death was an accident, but I've never thought so. Now with all the similarities between these two cases—" She quickly held up six fingers again to remind Rick of the count. "I'm thinking solving the Nolan case is the key to solving the Baker case.

"You'd be making a good argument, if both cases were murders."

Rita unfurled her legs, stretching them out in front of her. Her feet barely reached the coffee table. "Both of them had to be killed by somebody who could move a body." She talked faster, her pitch rising. "Not just physically move it, but transport it a long distance A kid couldn't do that."

"Yes—" Rick drew the single word out.

"But it doesn't add up. If an adult man killed Baker, he'd be old now, we're talking geriatric." She paused, and then began again with less enthusiasm. "Whoever killed Nolan would have to be quick and strong enough to subdue a teenager and break his neck."

"Keep going," Rick said. "It's kind of cute, you trying to punch yourself out of that paper bag." He leaned back in a relaxed posture again.

Rita kicked her foot in the direction of his knee, but didn't connect. "You think you're so smart," she said.

"Oh now, don't feel bad. I do the same thing all the time; follow an argument until I find the break in the logic. It's basic police work."

Rita picked her glass up and took a long swallow. That fancy wine was beginning to taste almost as bitter as her defeat.

"What about this?" Rick said. "What if our current suspect killed Nolan, we don't know how, but he wanted it to look like an accident. First he thinks about putting the bike and the body on the tracks beneath the overpass, but something changes his mind, maybe somebody nearby. So he loads the kid up in his car—the bike won't fit—and takes him out to the river, where he throws the body over the side of the bridge."

"I suppose that would be possible."

"Right. Then in one of those *couldn't do this if you were trying* moments, the kid's head lands dead center in a crotch of the tree branches like a freakin' hole-in-one at the golf course, and the momentum of his body snaps his neck!"

She could see Rick's struggle to keep a straight face.

"Of course, if this is the same guy that killed Baker, he's pushing seventy or better. In which case I think we'd have found him laying there on the bridge, dead from heart failure."

Rita threw a pillow at him. "Not funny," she said. "Seventy isn't *that* old. Hell, fifteen years ago my grandfather was still working out with a punching bag, and I can tell you I wouldn't have wanted to be on the receiving end of his right cross."

The words were out of her mouth before their full impact struck her. She felt a sinking in her chest. A doubt she'd never had about her grandfather's character twisted in the pit of her stomach. She wondered if her father had known what Pops's punch felt like? Until today, she'd never thought much about what it might have been like to be Pops's only son, to have to live up to those expectations.

She had to admit that growing up in a small town where everybody knew her grandfather was a mixed bag of curses and blessings. Aunt Sue said being a cop's daughter killed her dating life. She joked about never landing a boyfriend until she went away to Madison for college, where nobody knew who Dave Sullivan was.

For Rita, it was her grandfather's reputation that followed her everywhere she went. He'd been a good, benevolent cop, and a respected man even long after he left the force. The worst scolding Rita could ever receive from any adult when she was growing up was a simple reminder of how disappointed Pops would be if she screwed up.

And they all knew it worked too, from Grandma Abby to every last teacher she had. Even if all she did was fail to volunteer for some good deed or crappy detail, she'd hear it. *Your grandfather is going to be so disappointed in you.*

It was a mantra etched in her brain like grooves in a record, and the needle was stuck. It was the reason for Rita's overwhelming and persistent desire to always please her grandfather.

Maybe *that* was the catalyst for her obsession with the Baker case. She knew failing to make an arrest or get a conviction was Pops's greatest disappointment in himself. Solving it would be redemption for him, and accolades for her.

Maybe there'll even be a little redemption in it for me, she thought.

"Nobody messed with Dave Sullivan when he was on the force," Rick said. "That's the word, anyway. But still working out with a punching bag at seventy years old? Come on."

"For your information, my uncle still lifts weights everyday," she said. And did you know I have two great aunts in their 80s? They're both as healthy as horses."

"So it's possible that a man of at least seventy, or one of your octogenarian aunties, could toss a dead body into the river." Rick was nodding his head. "Just food for thought. How do you know both boys didn't die where the bodies were found, no foul play?"

"Listen, Rick. Sean Nolan sure as hell didn't fall off his bike, smack his head and then walk in a daze three miles to the Nemadji River where he fell down the embankment to his death."

"Okay, what about the Baker boy?" Rick asked.

"Found lying in the ditch on the road to the refinery. Did you know there was some lame theory that he crouched down on his skateboard and grabbed the back bumper of a passing car, and was flung into the ditch?"

"Bumper cruising; a lot of kids did it. And, yes, I have read the file, Rita."

Rita's pulse quickened. She wanted at that file so bad it made her ache, but every request she'd attempted was denied. "Baker's skateboard was at the church," she said. "How could he have been riding it on that road, latched onto a bumper or not?"

"People get too attached to what looks like a fact. Have you ever considered that the killer deliberately *left* Baker's skateboard at the church to throw people off? For that matter, who's to say that kid wasn't killed during the night—a JonBenét Ramsey situation? The guilty party dumps the body on the refinery road and then plants the skateboard back at the church."

"Somebody in his own family? That ugly rumor has been making the rounds for fifty years," Rita said. "Are you telling me you think it's true?" She still bristled at hearing that one. It couldn't be that simple. There had to be more to it.

"I'm saying you have to think of every possibility. Evidence isn't always what it seems on the surface. Anybody could have planted that skateboard outside the church before early mass."

Rita sat up, a burst of new excitement hitting her. "You're right. You're absolutely right."

"Well there's something I don't hear coming out of your mouth very often."

"What if it was more than one man?"

"I'm not sure I follow," Rick said.

"What if it was two men, or more precisely, a man and a boy that killed Baker? That boy could be as young as sixty right now, perfectly capable of killing Nolan and tossing him over a bridge." Her words tumbled out, her pitch rising again. "And what about this. If Baker was just hanging around the church, riding his board before mass and somebody came by in a car, trying to lure him, wouldn't he be much more likely to get in if there was another kid, maybe even a kid he knew?"

"So your theory is this hypothetical kid is repeating his mentor's crime on its anniversary." Rick weighed the theory. "I don't know Rita, you've churned out so many scenarios I can't keep them straight. What you don't have is motive."

"So, you admit it wasn't an accident?" Rita said.

"No. I'm saying you don't have a motive for murder. The motive for covering up an accidental death is easy—to save your ass." He smiled at her. His cheeks rounded up and out, forcing his eyes to nearly close.

"Why? I just don't get why everybody accepts that Baker's death was an accident, and some poor schmuck was just trying to cover it up."

"Maybe the poor schmuck was still on a Saturday night drunk, driving home before dawn. He hit Baker out on that road and just left him there. Might not've even remembered it after he'd slept it off."

"Because Baker was just standing there on the side of the road, bent over with his head perfectly lined up to a car bumper? Come on Rick, besides the blow to the head, he had no other injuries. And how would some stranger know enough to dump the Baker's skateboard at Immaculate Heart?" She asked. "Now who's grasping at unlikely theories?"

"We both are, Rita. It's late, the wine bottle's empty, and we're both tired."

She treated him to a withering gaze. "The only common thread between these two kids is Immaculate Heart. They both disappeared from that church and they both turned up dead. It doesn't take a rocket scientist or a good night's sleep to figure out somebody at that church was part of both crimes."

"Okay, I surrender. You win. Can we talk about something else now?"

"What's the best way to go about locating somebody?" she asked.

"What?" Rick asked. He rubbed his eyes with the thumb and forefinger of one hand. "Sorry, but trying to follow you isn't always easy–right now, it's damn near impossible."

"You know, like somebody who lived here, then moved," she said.

"Why do I get the feeling you're not really asking me how to do it? You want me to do it for you, huh?"

"Will you?" she asked with an ascending note of hope in her voice.

"Nope. But if it were me sitting over there being all snoopy reporter about this, I'd start by checking with relatives for a forwarding address."

"There are no relatives to ask. I'm talking about those priests they shuffled out of here, the two that were molesting boys."

"Then I guess you'd have to ask at the diocese office. But I'll save you the time. Both of the priests were questioned about the Baker boy after the allegations against them came out. Both were cleared of any connection to the case."

"What about a Father Bartoelli?" Rita asked. "He's never been accused of sexual abuse, but they hustled him out of here not long after the Baker boy was killed."

"Never heard of him. Listen, you're getting hung up on correlation and not causation," Rick said. "There are hundreds of members attending Immaculate Heart. Just because two boys from the same church go missing and end up dead, that isn't a guarantee there's a connection."

He rubbed his eyes again, this time with the palms of both hands. "And listen to me. You dragged me right back into this pointless conversation."

"Yes, listen to yourself. This is Superior, Wisconsin, population twenty-seven thousand. Homicides don't happen here every day. These two both have something to do with that church, or somebody there. What *else* do Baker and Nolan have in common, fifty years apart?" Rita asked.

"That's the million-dollar question." Rick said. "And when you can answer it, you'll have your killer."

Rita let her head fall back against the stack of pillows. She stared up at the ceiling, letting out a deep, long sigh. What, or who, did the two boys have in common. "Oh my God." She sat up, her eyes wide open and fixed on Rick.

"What?" he asked. "What are you thinking?"

The thoughts hit her fast and hard, like high waves pounding against the break wall at the Superior entry, slamming into her brain one right after another. Jim Wiese–Father Jim–went to Immaculate Heart. And he turned up back in Superior, at the church the same day another boy goes missing from there?

Her chest throbbed painfully. She realized she was holding her breath, "Jim." His name flowed out of her mouth on her breath, like a pressure valve released.

"Jim? Jim who?" Rick asked.

"Father Jim. Former addict turned priest. He was a year ahead of my dad in school, at Immaculate Heart. He would have been, what?" She tried to do the math in her head. "Maybe a high school senior when the Baker Boy was murdered."

"At Immaculate Heart?"

"Yes." Rita thought a moment. "Could be. I'm not sure. Immaculate Heart used to go all the way through high school, but I don't know when that changed."

"Rick sat up. "The same Father Jim that's at Immaculate Heart now?"

"Yes." Now she'd done it. After all the years she'd thought about the Baker case, after reading and rereading every newspaper article and pestering every cop she could, much to her grandfather's embarrassment, after wondering the whole time how a case could go so cold so fast–was the answer going to be this easy? More importantly, was it going to be one she didn't want?

"And you think this Father Jim had some connection to the Baker boy?" Rick asked. "Never mind. I don't want to hear any more of your wild theories. I'm going to have to interview him now and I'd prefer to do it with a clear head." He got up from the sofa and stood for a moment, looking around her apartment. "I'd better get going–the girls."

His daughters. The other reason they kept their relationship under wraps.

She watched him retrieve his clothes in the reverse order of the way he'd shed them: dark blue pants thrown over the arm of a side chair near the sofa, white shirt hanging off a stool shoved against the island that separated her kitchen from the living room, and the black, thick-soled shoes he'd kicked off at the door. His socks and boxers were in the bedroom.

"Yeah," she said. "I need to get to sleep; five-thirty comes around pretty fast."

"For me too," he said.

She watched him retreat up the short hallway. When he left her apartment, the cut-off sweats would be hanging on the back of the bedroom door, waiting for his next visit. They had the routine down.

Then why does it still feel so awkward? Rita wondered.

It wasn't his marital status; that was a technicality. Lying to his daughters didn't exactly sit well with her, but that was his sin, not hers. The fact was, she hadn't once asked him to spend the night and he hadn't once suggested it. No matter how she looked at it, not yet divorced or conflict of interests, it seemed they both knew theirs was a relationship with no foreseeable future.

VIII

Rita squinted at the bright morning sunlight bouncing off her windshield. She angled the rear-view mirror down to see her reflection. Crows feet framed her narrowed eyes like fine spider webs. She felt old, and she looked it. The bags under her eyes were as big and dark as two wedges sliced from a bruised plum.

She hadn't slept well at all, though not for lack of trying. As soon as Rick left she'd filled a tumbler full of ice and covered the ice with gin, topping it off with a splash of tonic.

Nothing wrong with a nightcap, she'd thought. A few more opinions piped up in her head, all of them critical—drinking too much, drinking alone, drinking to help her sleep. None of them were loud enough to stop her.

When the gin hadn't worked, she'd tried popping a few Tylenol. It was no use. She'd lain awake beneath her rumpled sheets for more than an hour. Like the trains rumbled through North End all night, her thoughts just kept rolling down the same track—trying to make a connection between Sean Nolan and Thomas Baker.

Rick was right about one thing. She was letting common knowledge of sexual abuse in the Catholic Church lead her to the easiest conclusions. Why wouldn't she, with two accused priests both serving the Immaculate Heart parish when Baker was killed?

She'd listened to all of Aunt Sue's recriminations and studied the photos of her father offered as evidence. He was an adorable little boy with a head full of dark curls framing his cherubic face, like a chubby Botticelli, except for the twinkle of mischief in his eyes. Then, about the time he was thirteen, the bright eyes and impish grin disappeared. To Rita, his expression had a desperate quality, like the photos of homeless souls living on the streets, or refugees with no country, their penetrating gaze searching for hope beyond the camera lens.

After talking to Father Jim, Rita wondered if there might be another reason for her father's disconsolate stare, one Aunt Sue didn't want to believe. Was it possible Sue clung to the suspicion that a priest molested her brother, so she could absolve her own father for physical abuses?

Pops's reluctance to talk about his only son seemed almost a dictate for others in the family to follow, but Rita always thought it was Pops's grief that kept him silent. The idea that he'd mistreated his own son—that they were a family silenced by dysfunction—was a new wrinkle, one that rippled into bumpy terrain as Rita's sleepless hours had mounted through the night.

Could it also be possible that Pops's reticence whenever she brought up the Baker case was the same? Was he hiding something? *Follow the argument until it doesn't make sense anymore.*

What if Jim killed Thomas Baker—an accident like Pops suggested? Then did Jim tell his best friend? Would two scared boys tell one of their fathers, the father who happened to be a cop? It didn't seem likely. But what if Pops found out on his own? Would he protect Jim?

There was only one answer to the question, no matter how abhorrent. Rita's father and Jim were best friends; if Jim was involved, so was her own father. It was the only reason Pops would protect *anybody*. It would explain why he quit the force. It could even be the reason that Rita's dad became sullen and withdrawn, started using drugs. It might even explain her father's death.

Jesus, what can of worms have I opened?

Rita swiveled the mirror back up, carefully adjusting the angle to center her line of sight between the backseat headrests. She'd tried removing them, to give herself a wider view out the rear window, but it turned out they weren't optional. She guessed the safety experts believed people in the back seat deserved protection from whiplash too.

"Idiots," she mumbled. There was never anybody in her backseat. She should have the option to take out her own damn headrests in her own damn car.

She shoved a pair of dark, sunglasses with large, thick frames onto her face. They helped with the sun that was burning her eyes out of their sockets, but not so much with the throbbing in her head. She backed cautiously onto 12th Street, and then pulled forward to the stop sign where she paused before darting across Hammond Avenue.

Rita pulled into the cul-de-sac parking on 14h Street, blocked from Tower Avenue to all but foot traffic. She nabbed the last vacant slot in the double row of parked cars. After more than a year she was accustomed to the new, smaller *Telegram* office on the ground floor of the New York building, but the parking situation continued to unnerve her daily. It would be easier to just walk the half mile to work, if she didn't need her car to go out on stories.

Her stomach was churning, her head was pounding, and she wanted nothing more than to go inside and lose herself in the day's tasks. She knew Rick was going to go to Immaculate Heart to talk to Father Jim. He'd make the connection between Jim and Rita's father. After that, Rick would go straight to Pops.

She shut the engine off. "Pops would never cover up a murder, even if his own son was involved." Rita hoped saying it out loud would convince her it was true.

She spent most of the morning wrapping up stories for the Friday edition. The phone call came just after noon. She let it ring when she saw Pops's I.D. come up on the display. It would be soon enough to face the music when she saw him after work. Thursday night was their standing dinner date. Sometimes they went out, but mostly Pops had dinner ready to serve when she got there. He didn't mind cooking so much when he knew he wouldn't be eating alone.

She knew Pops would keep calling until she answered. She picked her phone up and shot off a quick text:

`On a story right now. CU4 dinner.`

It was just before six when she knocked on Pops's door—third floor of the Phoenix Villa in the renovated St. Mary's Hall. St. Mary's had been one of Superior's first hospitals, now long since closed.

"Did you get any of the messages I left you today?" It was the first thing out of Pops's mouth when he opened the door to let Rita in.

"I didn't listen to them, Pops. You know Thursday are busy for me."

She went straight to the kitchen setting the bottle of wine she brought as a peace offering on the counter. She opened the drawer where Pops kept his corkscrew. The kitchen was small and organized, like the rest of his apartment in the senior complex. It was a compact, efficient little place. Small and orderly, for an older person's shrunken, quiet life, a place for everything and everything in its place.

She opened the bottle, rinsed the synthetic cork and dropped it into the decorative glass jar on the counter, Grandma Abby's jar of corks. The container had been filled and emptied into a larger box many times over many years. When the stoppers were still made of real cork, she and Grandma once used more than a hundred of them making a bulletin board to hang in Rita's bedroom. The two of them made coasters for beverages and trivets for pans hot off the stove. They even made silent wind chimes once, first painting the corks in bright colors and then dipping them in glue and glitter. Grandma had meant them to be a joke, something to amuse Rita, but they were actually very Zen, moving with the gentlest breeze and catching the light in shiny, multicolored glitter bits.

When Grandma died, Rita and Pops just kept saving the corks like always. When he moved from the old house overlooking Central Park a few years ago, Grandma's jar came with. Now when they filled it, they recycled the corks appropriately.

Whenever Rita looked back on her childhood, being raised by Pops and Grandma Abby didn't seem that unusual. They were young grandparents, Pops then forty-five and Grandma not yet even forty-three when Rita had gone to live with them. She'd had friends in school whose parents were around that age.

She walked over to the dining table. Pops had set it as usual with Grandma's white china, unadorned except for the narrow band of silver around the edges. Her plain-handled knives, forks, and spoons with the soft silver glow of brushed stainless steel were laid beside each plate atop a neatly folded paper napkin.

Pops took great care with the dishes and flatware, washing *and* drying them almost immediately after each use, then stacking them in the cabinet. He slipped layers of flattened coffee filters between the plates to minimize scratches. He assured Rita the complete set would be hers, someday. Pops just couldn't let them go yet.

Rita was surprised to see three settings. "Is Uncle Stan joining us?" Maybe Pops wasn't going to give her what-for after all.

Stan was a loner. He'd been married once, for a short time but it didn't suit him. More to the point, it didn't suit his wife. He'd met her when he was on leave in San Francisco. After he went back to 'Nam, they corresponded for the remainder of his tour. When Stan was discharged, they were married. When she divorced him a few years later, she took their baby daughter with her. Stan never tried to keep in touch.

"Stan's bringing sarma," Pops said.

Stan's sarma was legendary in the family. It was because of the home-brined cabbage he used to make the Croatian-style cabbage rolls.

"I made boiled potatoes; maybe you can mash them the way your Grandmother did, with butter and milk?"

"Sure, Pops," Rita said. One thing about Pops, in his eyes nobody could compare to Grandma Abby in the kitchen, he believed she had a special touch—even for the simplest things like mashed potatoes. "I wish I had known Uncle Stan was coming; I only brought one bottle of wine." Rita poured the deep red Burgundy into two of Pops's squat, cut-crystal tumblers and sat down.

Pops sat in the chair opposite of Rita. "What the hell have you been telling that detective you're sleeping with?"

So he was going to have it out with her before Uncle Stan arrived, and he wasn't holding anything back. He'd just fired both barrels right off the bat: You've been whoring around *and* telling tales out of school, Rita dear.

"I didn't tell him anything, exactly," she answered.

"Well, you dang sure told him enough."

Pops had never cursed around Rita or her grandmother, instead relying on softer euphemisms. *Dang* and *gosh darn* it were favorites. But his verbal restraint didn't mean he didn't get angry. He did, and he was now, she could tell.

"That's what comes of this nosing around in the Baker case. How many times have I told you to just let it go?"

"Enough times. You've told me more than enough times, Pops."

"Well, I guess it *wasn't* enough was it?"

"So what? What if Detective Drake knows that Jim was around when the Baker boy was killed, or that since he's come back to town another boy went missing and turned up dead? Why would you care, Pops? Is there something you aren't telling me?"

The doorbell rang.

"That'll be Stan," Pops said. "He's probably got his hands full."

Rita got up to open the door. Sure enough, Stan stood there holding a cardboard box from the grocery store. A kitchen towel was draped over the top.

"I hope I'm not late," he said, stretching his neck and head over the box. He was a tall drink of water, as Grandma Abby used to say, so the reach was easy for him. It was Rita's signal to kiss him on the cheek. She barely made contact when she did.

"I hit nearly every red light on the way over here. I don't know why you had to get a place in this building, Dave. You lived in East End all your life, you should be in my building."

"I was raised in the North End, remember? Same place as your mom. She moved to the East End when she married up. And for your information, Abby and I lived in Central Park—not East End.

"Oh, excuse me. I forgot that a few blocks make all the difference. Besides, you know what I meant. Claire and Katherine are still living there. It's more convenient."

Claire and Katherine were Pops's remaining siblings. Sophie, Stan's mother, Edward and Peter had all passed.

"Convenient for who?" Pops asked. "I'm closer to Rita over here and I like being downtown. That makes this building convenient for me."

"You've got a roaster full of sarma in that box, Uncle Stan, I can smell it." Rita interrupted what could easily become a lengthy debate between the two men.

"Sure, sure." The words came in rhythm with Uncle Stan's slight facial tic, a spasm of the muscles in his neck that pulled at one corner of his mouth. Aunt Sue told Rita he'd had the tic since he was a child. She said it explained a lot about Stan's social awkwardness.

Uncle Stan wasn't a bad guy—he was actually still quite handsome for 68 and he had a decent style—for a bachelor. Boot-cut jeans that fit snugly instead of bagging below his butt, breaking neatly over leather boots, knock offs of Born lace-ups. A far more stylish choice, in Rita's opinion, than the expected motorcycle or cowboy boots favored by half the men in Douglas County—the half not wearing work boots.

Instead of t-shirts or polos he wore button down shirts and a vest. He usually finished the look with a black leather coat, button front, like the one Stallone wore in the Rocky movies. For formal occasions, he added a tie to the ensemble.

Rita took the box from him. "Come on in and pour yourself some wine; you're going to need it. I'm in the dog house." She set the box on the kitchen counter, removed the towel, and lifted the roaster out. The aroma of ground lamb and beef, heavily seasoned with garlic, set Rita's stomach growling.

Uncle Stan was at her side, moving the box out of the way so she could set the roaster down. "I think it needs to be plugged in so it can warm up for a while." He leaned close, whispering in her ear. "You might want to skip the wine and go right to the slivo," he said.

Slivovitz, high-octane plumb brandy, the drink of her people, Rita called it. "So you've talked to Pops?" She spoke in the same whisper.

He nodded.

"What did he tell you?" She looked at Uncle Stan, trying to read his eyes, gauging how serious the situation might be. She didn't like the concern she saw there. "Never mind. I don't think I want to know."

"What are you two mumbling about in there?" Pops asked. "Come sit in here."

When they were all around the table, Rita spoke first. "Just so you know, Pops, I haven't talked to Detective Drake today. I have no idea what he's done, or who he's talked to since I saw him last."

"Me. He talked to me, probing like a dang cattle prod—asking everything I could remember about the Baker case. I didn't appreciate it. Not one bit."

"I'm beginning to wonder why, Pops. All these years I've thought you'd want the case solved. It's starting to sound an awful lot like you don't."

"Just tell her, Dave. If you don't, she's not going to leave it alone until she digs up the truth," Uncle Stan said. "On her own or with the help of that cop. And it won't be good, not for any of us."

IX

Uncle Stan's warning twisted a knot it Rita's stomach. Her hands began perspiring. All of her suspicions—no, her fears—from the night before filled her head at once. "Tell me *what*? What's he talking about, Pops?"

In the silence that followed, she felt her stomach lurch. She'd never seen Pops look so defeated, like he'd lost—everything. "Pops, what is it?" she asked.

When he still didn't speak, Rita prompted him, hoping to hear the lesser of the two evils she imagined. "Pops, did Jim Wiese kill Thomas Baker? Are you protecting him?"

"No, Rita. I'm not protecting Jim."

Rita looked from Pops's face to Uncle Stan's. His tic was working double time. She looked back at Pops, and the nausea in her stomach rose up to her gullet. She pushed her wine glass away.

"Rita, I never wanted to tell you this. I never wanted to tell anybody." His words caught in throat. He reached for his wine glass and took a big swallow.

"Pops?"

"I believe your father was the one who killed Thomas Baker—and I deliberately withheld knowledge that might have proved it."

Rita pushed her chair back from the table. She felt a hot flush begin in at her chest and flow up to her face. Hear ears started to buzz and her vision narrowed. She dropped her head in her hands and willed herself not to faint. "I don't believe it. That can't possibly be true."

Stan interceded. "Rita, you have to hear him out."

She put her head on the table, trying to make sense of the words that wouldn't come together in any coherent thought. It was no use. "Why?" she asked.

"I don't know," Pops said. "Out of his mind on that psychedelic crap, all those pills he was taking—and who knows what else."

Rita lifted her head. "Come on, Pops, what was he, fifteen?"

"Sixteen, when the Baker boy was killed. But the first time your father overdosed on that poison he wasn't much beyond fifteen. If he hadn't vomited his guts out he would have died then. It was the first time your grandmother and I had to take him into emergency."

Rita looked at Stan. "Uncle Stan, is this true? I know Grandma blamed you—she said you were the one that got him hooked when you came back from Vietnam. Did you?"

"I was no saint, Rita, that's for sure, but I was gone when all of this went down. I joined the Navy at seventeen. I lied about my age, and I was such a head case, I re-upped after my first tour. Anyway, I didn't have to teach your father anything about drugs when I got back. He already knew what he was doing."

"Your grandmother had to have somebody to blame, Rita." Pops said. "She coddled the boy, always protected him too much. He was weak; that's why he took drugs."

Rita's pulse pounded; her anger seemed as uncontrollable as the blood surging through her veins. "And is that why you beat him, because he was weak?" If Rita thought her grandfather looked defeated a few minutes ago, she didn't know it by half. He seemed to wither right before her eyes, looking every bit as old as his 86 years. "Father Jim told me," she said.

"I was too hard on him, yes. Maybe your grandmother was trying to compensate for that. I just wanted him to straighten up and be a man. The only thing he was interested in was getting hopped up on drugs."

"So how did he kill the Baker kid? How did my sixteen-year-old father bash in Thomas Baker's skull and then dump his body all the way out on the refinery road?"

"He was crazy when he was on that crap, Rita. I don't know what he might have been capable of."

"What do you mean, you don't know? If you don't know that, how do you even know he killed Baker?"

"I don't, not with a hundred percent certainty." He held up his hand to stop her next question. "Your father was hanging out with the kids over at the college, draft dodgers, smoking their marijuana and popping their acid."

"Dropping."

Pops looked at her.

"It's dropping acid. You drop acid, you pop pills."

"Whatever they were dropping, popping, shooting up—they were dope heads."

"And?" Rita had her arms crossed over her chest in a defensive posture.

"And your father was listening to all of their garbage-talk, about protesting the war, how our soldiers were baby killers."

"A lot of that was true," Rita said. "Sorry, Uncle Stan."

Stan avoided her eyes. "Save your apologies. It wasn't pretty over there—none of it."

"Rita, your father and I were at opposite poles." Pops said. "I served in Korea. Stan was in Vietnam running missions in those Godforsaken swamps, and there was your father, telling me he wouldn't go if he *was* drafted. Said he'd hitchhike across the border into Canada, find a commune to live in up there—it would be easy, there were plenty of them." Pops took a breath. "I told him I wasn't raising a coward and he said—" Pops eyes teared up and he choked on his words.

Stan took over. "He told your grandfather that if killing somebody was what it took to prove he was a man, he didn't have to go to Vietnam to do it."

"That? That's it? Teenage posturing? I gotta hand it to you, that's some detective work."

"There's more, Rita." Uncle Stan said. "Your father and I grew up close, almost like brothers. We wrote letters back and forth the whole time I was in 'Nam. I really appreciated getting something regular at mail call. He asked me once if it was true that soldiers cut off the ears of their enemies and kept them. I told him I'd seen it, ears, noses, fingers," he hesitated. "And other parts."

"I'm not following," Rita said.

Pops cleared his throat, took a long swallow of his wine and then a deep breath. "You asked me in the restaurant Sunday if there was something the police held back—the detail that would help them know the real killer if he was ever found."

"Yes."

"Your father had run away again, he was gone for three or four days, I don't remember exactly. The same morning Thomas Baker went missing, Frankie showed up at home, higher than a kite and all banged up from putting his motorcycle in a ditch. When he collapsed I didn't know if it was from drugs or injuries. Your grandmother and I got him into the car and took him to emergency, again."

"They pumped his stomach, but it was the worst ever. They put him on IVs and admitted him for overnight observation. By the time he came home the next day, the Baker case had broken. You father couldn't remember a thing, where he'd been or what he'd done for days. Or at least, that's what he said." Pops's hands were on the table, folded and fidgeting. "And now you've got your detective boyfriend nosing around, asking me questions about the case."

"What does any of that have to do with what the police held back?" Rita asked.

"Later that week I went into the rectory office, the same as I always did, to help the church secretary, Mrs. Johnson, balance the books. I opened my briefcase and on top of my folders was a severed ear. Thomas Baker was missing his left ear when they found his body."

Rita's heart pounded so hard and fast it felt as though it was lurching up into her throat. Rising to her feet she strode into the kitchen and went straight to the cupboard where Pops kept the slivo. She poured a good-sized shot into the first glass she could find and drank it down in one swallow.

The slow burn started in her throat, traveled to her stomach and then back up again where it exploded in her chest. She took two more glasses from the cupboard extending one finger into each of the three, picking them up in a cluster. She grabbed the bottle with the other hand and headed back to the dining room. She sat down at the table and poured three shots, slamming hers down before speaking. Fire in the throat. Uncle Stan followed suit.

"Let me get this straight," Rita said. "You think my father killed Thomas Baker, but you don't know how and he never remembered doing any such thing. You're basing all of this on the fact that he heard stories about body parts and trophies. Who didn't back then, I know. And you also think he was trying to prove something? That he cut the Baker kid's ear off and put it in your briefcase? That's all of it?"

"I didn't know what to think, and with no facts to the contrary, your father could have been convicted on the circumstantial evidence."

"Only if somebody knew what he'd said to you. Jesus, Pops."

"I couldn't take that risk, Rita. If he said it to me, he probably repeated it to those damn hippies he was hanging around with."

"The knife," Rita said. "The goddamn knife. The killer probably used it to cut the ear off. It would have had fingerprints and Baker's blood on it. That's why the knife was such a big deal."

"If we'd found it, if we'd been able to lift prints, it might have cleared your father." Pops drank down the shot Rita had poured for him. "Or convicted him. I couldn't have protected him if that was the case, I wouldn't have."

"There's just one big goddamn gaping hole in your theory." Rita was yelling at her grandfather, something she couldn't remember ever doing before.

"Hey now, that's enough. Watch your language." Pops said.

Pops had let her first few curses slide, but she knew he wasn't going to let her keep it up without protest.

"You just accused my father of murder. I think I'm entitled to some strong language," she said.

Uncle Stan tried to smooth things over. "Dave, you knew she'd be upset. Cut her some slack." He reached for the bottle of liquor and poured another round of shots. "Rita, you don't know what this has done to your grandfather all these years."

"And you? You've known about this the whole time?"

"No." Stan shook his head. "I didn't know until after your father died. Your Pops and I, we had a little too much to drink, and it just came out."

Rita turned to her grandfather. "Pops, really, is this what you believe?"

"What else could I believe, Rita?"

"That maybe somebody else put that ear there?"

"Who, Rita? That briefcase was always either in my den at home, or with me at the church. Even if somebody else did have access, why? Why would they put that ear in my briefcase?"

"Oh, I don't know. Maybe the killer was one of those crazy war protestors he hung around with. You just said yourself that he likely bragged to his friends about the shit he told you. Maybe one of them was some whack-job veteran who came back from Vietnam with his head f—" Rita corrected her language. "Messed up. Or anybody who knew you'd automatically pin it on my dad. Did you ever consider any of that?"

"Consider it? I held onto it like a drowning man holding his last gulp of air. You know how many nights I laid awake, trying to clear my head of how Thomas Baker might have suffered?"

Rita felt her anger wavering.

"It didn't matter how much I tried to push the idea from my head, it made no sense at all for anybody else to cut off that poor boy's ear and then make sure I got it. You tell me. Who would do that?"

"We'll never know that now, since you withheld key evidence." Rita let her head drop back until it rested on the chair back. She stared up at the ceiling. "Where is it? What did you do with it?"

"The ear? I got rid of it, for cripes sake. I burned it, in the coal stove."

Rita remembered the black cast iron Royal Oak stove down in the basement of their Central Park house. Grandma used it to burn cardboard and paper. "You destroyed evidence in a homicide. You broke the law." Her tone was flat, without accusation. Her eyes didn't waver from the blank canvas of the low ceiling.

"Do you think I don't know that? He was my only son," Pops said.

Rita's fight came back. She lifted her head and looked at her grandfather. "He was *my* only father."

"Rita, I'm sorry. You can't know how hard it was, how hard it's been all these years. You don't understand. You don't have a child."

Rita felt the rage wash over her again. She wanted to kick something, break Grandma Abby's precious dishes, fling the crystal across the room, smashing every piece. "Oh, don't play the devoted father with me. I won't believe it any more. Father Jim told me all about the times you beat your son, so you don't get to judge me from on high."

"I never beat your father."

"Wait, what did Father Jim call it, knocking him around? Isn't that what all the fathers did then?"

"Rita I—"

"Save it. I don't want to hear any more of your excuses."

"Rita." Stan interrupted. He was shaking his head back and forth. "Your father never beat Frankie. Not even close."

"So that makes it okay? That he just slapped my father around a little bit? Didn't spare the rod?"

"A kid needs some discipline." Uncle Stan's twitch was working overtime.

"Don't try to feed me that bullshit."

"Rita, that's enough! There's no need to take this out on your Uncle Stan."

Rita turned her anger back to Pops. "Jim could have killed Thomas Baker and put that ear in your briefcase hoping you'd do exactly what you did—cover it up to protect your son."

"Holy shit," Stan said. "She could be right, Dave."

"You think I didn't consider it?" Pops asked. "I couldn't find out any more about what Jim Wiese was doing that morning than I could about your father. For all I know, they were together and that Baker kid could have tagged along with them for a joy ride. Your father couldn't even remember where he'd spilled his bike, or getting himself home on it afterwards—thanks to those danged drugs of his. And the Baker kid could have been in on that too. We didn't check blood for drugs back then."

Rita listened, focusing on every word of her grandfather's deduction. "Did you accuse my dad? Did you make him believe that he did it and couldn't remember? Is that why he finally killed himself with *those danged drugs of his?*"

She'd said it, *out loud.* Frank Sullivan had committed suicide. It was the most likely truth that nobody in her family ever wanted to admit, least of all Rita.

There was barely a trace of color left in Pops's face. His lips were ashen; even the brown of his eyes seemed faded. "I never told him what I suspected, Rita. I never told a soul except Stan, and not until after your father was gone, just like Stan said."

Rita shook her head, refusing to accept what she was hearing. "Has it crossed your mind in the last week, either of you, that it couldn't be my father who killed Thomas Baker because whoever did it killed Sean Nolan too? I would think you'd be the first to want to prove that."

"It has, and you don't know how much I want that to be true. It's also possible that somebody just wanted to make it *look* like Sean and Thomas were killed by the same person."

"The only thing those two boys have in common is that church. Why isn't anybody else thinking what I'm thinking? That it was a priest. Christ, everybody knows what they were doing behind those sacristy doors. Has it not occurred to you that maybe a priest is responsible for both murders?"

"Thomas Baker disappeared and was killed on a Sunday. I think the priests were probably all busy, don't you?" Pops said. "And there's not a single priest at Immaculate Heart now that was there fifty years ago."

"Father Jim was there fifty years ago," Rita said.

"He wasn't a priest then, he was still a kid."

"And so was my father, but you think he could have done it. And don't give me the line about it being an accident. Why the hell would my father cut off a kid's ear if it was an accident?"

"The drugs," Stan said.

Rita glared at him.

"I'm just saying Jim wasn't a priest," Pops said. "You were talking about priests molesting young men, and possibly killing them. You're getting yourself all mixed up. You're talking crazy, Rita."

Rita pushed her chair away from the table again. "I don't care; there's a connection. You're wrong about my father and I'm going to prove it. I can't believe you didn't try harder. And you're trying to prove to yourself now that you did."

She slid her chair away from the table and stood up, putting some effort into not swaying as her head suddenly worked at balancing all her weight with those shots of slivo hitting it. "What's worse, you destroyed evidence and quit the force." Rita fought the tears she felt threatening to spill over. She was more angry than sad. Her tears always came quicker with anger, and it made her look weak. She despised that. "I can't even think about all this right now. I have to go."

"Don't leave, Rita. Don't go like this, please." Pops begged her. "We haven't eaten. Stan brought sarma."

"You've got to be kidding me. I don't want to eat now."

"Let me fix some for you, take it with you. You'll be hungry later. You'll have to eat something."

"Pops, just stop! I don't want any damn sarma."

Her old mantra was playing in her head, like a broken record again. *Your grandfather would be so disappointed in you.*

All these years I've felt inferior to your goddamn standards," she said. "What a joke." She hesitated before landing the final blow. "I'm just so disappointed in *you*, Pops." Her tears were flowing freely now, and she wiped them away quickly. She wanted Pops to know she was furious with him, not weak, not broken.

Whatever he thought, she'd hit the mark. She watched his chest sink. His face visibly sagged, the lines around his mouth and on his forehead deepened. Rita felt a pang of remorse, but at the same time she didn't care.

He'd lied to her; he'd been lying to her all these years.

She felt as if she'd split into two people. One of them was busy denying everything her grandfather had just said, outraged that he could even *think* his own son had killed Thomas Baker. *Her father.* The other Rita believed it, crushed beneath the weight of the one truth in all of it: Her Pops, a man she'd always looked up to and even envied for his uncompromising integrity, was fallible after all.

It was the enraged Rita who stomped to the door, yanked it open and slammed it on her way out. In the elevator she fished her phone out of her purse and pressed the speed dial for Rick. He answered on the third ring.

"Rita. I'm glad you called. We need to talk."

"Damn straight we need to talk. Meet me at the Spirit Room. I'll be there in five minutes." She hung up before he could protest.

Outside Pops's building, Uncle Stan's prized El Camino was parked right in front of her. She nearly clipped the rear fender pulling out around it. To her knowledge, it hadn't suffered so much as a scratch in the original gold paint since the day he bought it of the showroom floor at the old Larson Chevrolet. He treated it as though the paint was 24-karat and the chrome was solid platinum.

Just what I don't need, smashing into Uncle Stan's car and a DUI on top of it. She eased back on the gas pedal and focused on getting to the Spirit Room without incident.

X

By the time Rick arrived at the Spirit Room, Rita was already into her second gin and water—tall. She was sitting at the corner table, watching for him. Sun streamed in through the tall, arched windows of the historic Trade and Commerce Building. Rick sat down in the chair opposite her, with his back to the window. "Rita, I shouldn't be in here; I'm still on duty."

The bartender came with another tall glass, filled with clear liquid over ice. "One ice water." She smiled at Rick. "I'm guessing this is yours?"

"You guessed wrong," Rita said. "Bring one more, please."

The girl lost her smile. "Sure thing," she said.

Rick waited until she was out of earshot before talking to Rita again. "If you're ordering ice water chasers, that isn't your first gin and tonic tonight."

"Not tonic—water. Gin and water."

"Oh boy. What else have you had?"

She had to admit that despite the minimal time they spent together in public, Rick knew her habits, and he knew that whenever she switched to plain water for a mix, she was on a roll.

"Well, let's see. I started out with a glass of wine before dinner with Pops. We switched to something a little stronger after that."

"Listen Rita. I know you're probably upset with me, but I'm just doing my job."

She wanted to lay into him, but she was really starting to feel the booze. She reached across the table for the ice water the bartender put in front of Rick. "You don't mind, do you? She's bringing another."

"Be my guest," Rick said.

Rita drank half the glass, trying to get her thoughts straight in her head. She hadn't stuck around Pops long enough to find out what he'd told Rick, if anything, or what Father Jim had said. She put the glass down.

"I hear you talked to Father Jim today," she said. "And he told you that he and my father were best friends, so you went to talk to Pops."

"You seem angry about that. I was just following up on—"

"Yeah, yeah, I get that. What else did Jim have to say?"

"You know I can't tell you that."

Rita leaned over the table. "I don't care about the rules, Rick. I'm not interviewing you for the paper. I'm not going to report what you say."

"I think maybe we should talk about this somewhere else, someplace a little more private." Rick somehow managed to give her his full attention, while still scanning the room. It was a cop thing.

"Fine with me." Rita picked up her drink and drained the contents of the glass.

The bartender returned with the ice water. "Need another of those?" she asked.

"No, thanks. We're leaving." She slid to the edge of chair, standing up slowly.

"I've got this," Rick said, putting several bills from his wallet on the table. "Keep the change," he told the waitress. He followed Rita into the room-sized foyer outside the tapas bar.

"You know this used to be the courthouse, right?" Rita asked. "Right in these rooms. This is where they dispensed justice in this town, what there was of it." She pointed to the Spirit Room and its twin space across the hall, converted to a baking and food prep kitchen supplying both the bar and the Red Mug coffee house on the lower level.

"The courtrooms were on the second floor, Rita. I think this was the post office, or maybe a bank."

She ignored him. "The police station was right down those stairs. The police station my grandfather worked in. He was sitting in that station the night they found Thomas Baker. He was the desk sergeant on duty. Did he tell you that?"

"I knew that, Rita. You told me last night. Look, I don't want you driving home."

"I can walk. It's only a block if I cut across one lawn and then right up the alley behind the old library."

"Just give me your keys. I'll drive you home and then walk back to get my car."

"No, I'll walk. I need to blow off some steam."

"Give me your keys, then."

"What?"

"I know you. You'll walk out that back door and get right into your car, because it's only two blocks driving. What can happen in a few blocks, right?"

Rita felt the intensity of his pointed stare.

"Maybe we could ask Jane that question," he said. "Oh, wait. She wouldn't be able to articulate the details, would she?"

Jane was the wife. Not three years ago she was stopped at a red light waiting to make a left turn. She was on her way home after work, less than five blocks to go and she'd be in her brightly lit kitchen, preparing the night's meal for her husband and daughters. Instead, a drunk driver hit her from behind and pushed her car into the oncoming lane, where she was quite literally run over by a fully loaded semi-truck.

Jane survived, if you could call it that. They managed to stop all the internal bleeding and set all the broken bones, but after lying in a coma for nearly a month before regaining consciousness, she never really came back. Now she was living in a TBI facility—traumatic brain injury. She'd be there the rest of her life.

"You already have a wife to take care of, Rick. Stop trying to babysit me."

"You know what? Fuck you. Go out and get in your car. The minute you put that key in the ignition I'll arrest your ass."

"Fine! Follow me outside, then follow me all the way home if you want to, because I'm walking."

"Rita, what the hell is eating you? I only went to talk to your grandfather because I had a lead I needed to check out with somebody who'd worked the Baker case."

"What lead?"

Rick shifted his weight to one foot. He looked down at her, and then focused his gaze past her shoulder, looking out the wall of glass doors and windows facing Broadway Street. "Rita, it's not that I don't want to tell you."

"Yeah, I know. You can't." She stood there for a moment, contemplating her options before taking her chances. "Was Sean Nolan missing an ear when they found him?"

"Jesus Christ, Rita!" His eyes snapped back to her face. "Did your grandfather tell you that?"

"Then it's true?"

He grabbed her by the elbow and steered her to the door. "Outside," he said. His car was parked at the curb. He pushed her toward it.

"Let go of my arm," Rita said.

Rick ignored her, keeping a firm hold until she was standing by the passenger door. "Get in."

"What?"

"I said get in, we need to talk."

"Are you arresting me?"

"You know I'm not. Now get in." He repeated his command with less volume but more force, reaching to open the door as he did.

Rita got into the front seat. Rick slammed the door behind her. She waited for him to circle around the car and get in on the driver's side before she smarted off. "Okay, nobody can hear us now. I'm not wearing a wire, and it's your car, so you know it's not bugged. Are you going to answer my question?"

"A wire." Rick chuckled and shook his head. "That's a little dramatic, don't you think?"

"You're the one going all Hollywood cop on me," Rita said.

"Look, Rita, this isn't a game. Or if it is, you just changed the rules. I'm going to ask you again what you know. You can answer me here, in this nice friendly conversation we're having, or I can make it official if that's what you want."

"So you *would* arrest me?"

"Just answer my question. Did your grandfather tell you Thomas Baker was missing an ear?"

"Yes!" Rita was shouting now. "Yes, he told me that! And if Sean Nolan's missing an ear too, then it proves the same person's responsible for both deaths!"

"I'd say I was surprised your grandfather revealed confidential information, but I know how relentless you can be. I also know you could hound him into eternity and not get anything on the Nolan case because he doesn't *know* anything to tell, so you're guessing."

"Why do you have to be so stubborn?" she asked. "Why can't you just admit that these cases are almost identical?"

"Oh, I think you hold the record on stubborn. What I can't figure out is why any of this is so important to you. What is it you're not telling me? Why are you on a crusade to solve the Baker case?

"It's not a crusade," she said. That wasn't a lie, exactly. She'd certainly never thought of it as a crusade, just journalistic curiosity and, maybe, her own ego—a local reporter solving a fifty-year-old case. Until a few hours ago, that's all it had been.

Rita felt the tears coming on. She bit down hard on her tongue, trying to short circuit her emotions with pain. She turned her face away from Rick, looking out the passenger window, so he couldn't see she was crying.

"Rita, you've got to promise me that you won't tell anybody about the Baker kid, and the ear. I mean it, not a soul."

She didn't answer.

"Rita. I'm thinking about your own safety."

"I got it. I'm not going to tell anybody, okay?"

Rick started the engine and put the car in drive, his foot still on the brake. "I'm going to take you home. Eat something, have a cup of coffee, and then come back and get your car later."

She turned to face him. "Rick, you have to tell me. I can't tell you why I need to know, but I do." The shock, anger, and booze of the last hour all collected their due. Rita burst into tears. "Please, just tell me if the killer's signature was the same in both cases. Tell me if Sean Nolan's ear was cut off. I have to know."

Rick slid the transmission back into park.

"Rita, what is this? Do you think you know who the killer might be?"

"No." Rita shook her head back and forth, lips pressed tight to hold back her sobs. She couldn't tell Rick what she really wanted to hear from him: clear-cut proof that her own father *hadn't* killed Thomas Baker. She'd have to implicate Pops to explain it all to him. What Pops did was in clear violation of his sworn duty as an officer.

"Just take me home, Rick."

He dropped her off in her short driveway, more of an apron in front of the garage, next to the alleyway. She slammed the door when she got out, resisting the urge to open it and slam it again, about ten more times. She strode up the sidewalk to the back door of the old three-story house. She'd never used the front entrance in the entire time she'd lived in the apartment. It opened into a narrow hallway housing a stairway to the upper floor apartments, with the door to her apartment tucked under the far end. She didn't even know where she'd put the key to open it. The only time she set foot in the communal hallway was to pick up the mail the carrier dropped through the brass slot, sort it out by tenant names if she was the first to retrieve it, and put what wasn't hers on the small table against the wall.

She turned the key in the lock, pushing on the back door at the same time, nearly launching herself into her apartment. She stumbled across the room and dropped onto the sofa. She kicked her shoes off with enough force to sail them across the room, then propped her bare feet on the coffee table, pushing aside the clutter of mail and remote controls—one each for the TV, the Sirius radio, and the Roku that streamed her regular fix of Netflix and Hulu.

It was times like this Rita wished she smoked. She could swear she was having nicotine cravings, but that was impossible. She'd never been a smoker. Well, almost never. Trying a few drags with Billy Endicott when they were sitting in Central Park after dark didn't really count.

Maybe I smoked in a previous life, she thought. That was the only explanation she could come up with to account for her utter enjoyment of breathing in a second-hand puff from a good Marlboro. She'd never met anybody else with this unexplainable urge to inhale tobacco products when they'd never even smoked before.

Whatever it was, she wished she had a cigarette now. She bet it would take her mind off pillaging the cupboards for a forgotten candy bar or a few stale cookies.

Pops had called while she was still in the car arguing with Rick, and she had ignored the ringtone. She picked her phone up off the table where she'd dropped it and listened to the voice mail; he was worried. Rita tapped the screen to call him back. He answered on the first ring.

"Rita, are you okay? Are you home?"

"I'm home, Pops. I'm okay."

"You left here so angry. I've been worried about you. Did you get anything to eat?"

"I ate, Pops." She lied.

"Well, I just want to make sure you're okay," he said again. "You had some wine and two glasses of slivo."

"It's okay, Pops. I'm in for the night. I'm drinking some tea," she lied again. It wasn't that Pops tried to control her life—okay, maybe he did, a little. Pops could be over-protective sometimes, but the bottom line was he cared about Rita and she knew it.

The phone silence stretched a little too long for comfort. Rita broke it. "I talked to Rick—Detective Drake. He said Jim gave him a lead and that's why he wanted to talk to you, to somebody who had been on the force when Thomas Baker was killed. Do you know what it was?"

"A lead? He didn't say anything about a lead, specifically."

"What did he ask you?"

"He wanted to know what was happening at Immaculate Heart fifty years ago. How well did I know the priests? Who else was there on a regular basis? Were there any employees like janitors, or parishioners who did other jobs?"

"What did you tell him?"

"I told him there were a lot of people in the altar societies who came and went, a janitor and a secretary. I had to tell him I was doing the books. He seemed especially interested to know if I remembered anybody who stood out or caught my attention. He asked if I knew who made the anonymous donation for the holy water font."

Rita had never thought to ask Pops that, but then she never really knew he'd been helping with the parish books. "*Did* you know?"

"No, it was cash in a plain envelope. Put in the collection plate if I remember correctly. There was a note explaining it was for the font."

"And that was all? He didn't ask you anything else?"

"It was enough. He's suspicious about something, and you say Father Jim gave him a lead?"

"Yes. Are you sure he didn't ask you about Father Jim, specifically?"

"No, but he asked about Father Bartoelli."

"The priest who left suddenly?"

"Yes, him."

"What did you tell him?"

"He was one of three or four priests at Immaculate Heart. Didn't seem different from any of the rest. Nobody thought much of it when he left. The diocese reassigned priests all the time."

"Yes, little did anybody know why," Rita said. "Did he ask you about the ear?"

"No, Rita, and more the better. He'd only ask me if he was suspicious about it."

"Pops, I told him I know."

"You did what? When?"

"When I talked with him tonight, after I left your place. I was angry, I wanted him to tell me if Sean Nolan was missing an ear too. Pops, I'd bet my last meal that he was. The way Rick jumped out of his skin and came down all over me, it's the only explanation."

"So you just flat out told an officer that I revealed key details on an unsolved case. If you're right, and Nolan is missing an ear too, you've just put me in a bad spot. They could call me in for questioning, and I'm guessing their first question will be why I'd tell you—what the context of our conversation was."

"Tell them I'm a nosy reporter."

"Geez Rita, think! That would only make it worse. You're the last person on earth I should be shooting my mouth off to."

"You're old, Pops. If they ask you anything, just play the confused card."

"Rita, you're going to be the death of me."

It wasn't the first time she heard that—not by a long shot.

XI

It was past nine-o'clock. There wouldn't be anybody in the rectory office at this time of night, but what if there were an emergency? What if somebody needed last rites or something? There had to be an answering service or emergency line.

She called 4-1-1 for the number to Immaculate Heart and waited while the service connected her. The call went straight to voicemail giving an emergency number, just as she expected. She jotted it down, but wasn't anxious to dial. It would likely connect her to Father Carmichael–not the person she wanted to talk to.

She decided to drive to the rectory, but first she'd have to get her car. Outside, the cool evening air helped to clear the alcohol-fueled fog in her head, at least a little. She picked up her pace. Rick had all the same information she did and more resources at his disposal. And now, she'd stupidly blabbed about Pops letting her in on the Baker kid's missing ear. Rick would go back to Father Jim with new questions. Rita wanted to talk to him first.

She drove along the bayfront with the bug's top down–more fresh air blowing at her face. There was always a pack of wintergreen gum in the cup holder of her console, and she popped two pieces in her mouth to kill the taste of alcohol. She shouldn't be driving, but if she didn't go now, she might not have the guts in the morning. She was on her way to talk to a man she believed might be a cold-blooded killer. Besides, she had to get to Father Jim before Rick talked to him again. His story might change after that.

The glow of the setting sun angled across Barker's Island, striking the tall masts of the sailboats moored in the marina. It all looked so peaceful. Rita wished she were on one of those boats, feeling the gentle rocking of the waves, sitting on the deck with a better view of the sunset than the little bit getting caught in the corner of her rear view mirror.

One of those boats belonged to Mark. She tried to slam the door on the thought, but it already had a foot in. Her eyes scanned the masts, the fiberglass and wood hulls, wondering which one belonged to her ex-husband and his new wife. It would be easy enough to find out, but she'd resisted that particular mania–so far. *Local reporter arrested on charges of stalking. News at ten.*

She drove on, swallowing the green bile of envy that rose in her throat, ruminating on her list of regrets. The boat, the house in Billings Park, the untarnished life—a family, all the things she'd been divested of as her punishment for failing at happily ever after.

She parked on the street in front of the Immaculate Heart rectory. Father Carmichael answered the door when she rang the bell.

"Ms. Sullivan. Is there something I can do for you?" He tempered his question with a raised hand that signaled her not to speak too soon. "As long as you're not here to inquire further about the Nolan boy. If that's the case, I'm afraid I won't oblige."

"I wanted to talk to Father Jim, if I could."

Father Carmichael regarded her for a long moment. She remembered that kind of intense scrutiny from her school days, with disapproval evident in the arch of brow and set of the jaw, making her feel guilty even when she'd done nothing wrong. She wondered if the guilt stare was part of their training for priesthood, and for the nuns too. They certainly all had it down to a science.

"Come inside. I'll see if he's available."

Father Carmichael disappeared through an open doorway while Rita waited in the narrow foyer. She could hear the deliberately low conversation from the next room, but couldn't quite make anything out from their muffled voices. They stopped and Jim came in to greet her. "Rita. To what do I owe the pleasure?"

"I wanted to talk to you, if it's not too late."

"No, it's not at all. Come in." He gestured her through the doorway.

"In private, if we can."

"Certainly."

Rita had never seen the inside of the rectory, other than the reception room and office space she and Mark had visited for their marriage instruction. She stepped into a large room that didn't look much different from most typical living rooms, other than the dark wood-paneled walls and heavy fabrics from a bygone era. There was a large sofa and two side chairs arranged around three sides of a rectangular coffee table, a few potted plants, a radio sitting on a side table and a stack of bookshelves against one wall. No television.

Father Carmichael was nowhere in sight. Rita glanced though another doorway, leading into the next room. She could see the end of a dining table and a few of the chairs around it. She wondered if he was lurking there just out of sight, listening.

"I feel pretty special today, with all the visitors I'm receiving," Father Jim said.

"Detective Drake was here to see you."

"Good guess."

"Tonight?"

"No, earlier–this afternoon."

Rita drew on every instinct she'd developed as a reporter, trying to read Jim. She was in no hurry to talk, her first and best trick. Most people were uncomfortable with silence and eager to fill it. Usually what came out of their mouth in those moments told her a lot. Right now, she could be standing toe to toe with a murderer and she was *very* interested in what he had to say.

She felt Father Jim sizing her up too. Looking directly into her eyes, a slight smile on his face. "I think I see a lot of your father when I look at you," he said.

Rita was wise to him. He was trying to put her at ease, recreate a connection they shared through her father. "I don't look like my mother, at all?" she asked.

"Maybe a little, around the eyes. She was astute, like you. At least when she wasn't high on something."

It seemed a harsh comment, regardless of its truth. Rita said nothing.

"I'm sorry, where are my manners? Please, sit down. Can I get you anything to drink? I think we have some iced tea in the refrigerator."

"No, thank you," Rita said, taking a chair. Father Jim sat at the end of the sofa nearest her.

"Something stronger? Wine or a mixed drink?"

"No. No, nothing." Rita said.

"I'm curious Rita. Did you never try to find your mother?"

"No," she answered. "But she never came looking for me, either. I don't have a single memory of her. Pops and Grandma Abigail were my parents, I never felt a longing, or an empty hole, or whatever you think I should have."

Jim laughed. "And that is your grandfather coming out–tough as nails, as I remember."

Was this all just polite small talk, or was he trying to distract her? "Detective Drake told Pops you gave him a lead, something he had to check out with someone who'd worked the Baker case."

"He talked to your Pops?"

"Yes but Pops isn't clear on what lead you might have provided."

"Well, for starters he asked me a bunch of questions about what I was doing back in '66, if I'd still been attending school here, if I'd known Tom Baker, if I'd been an altar boy too, if we'd ever hung out together outside of church."

Rita's heart beat faster, her throat constricted. She swallowed several times, trying to generate enough saliva to moisten her dry mouth before she spoke again. "Did he ask you anything about Sean Nolan?"

"You put Drake on me didn't you? With a whole town full of people that were here then and still here now, you figured, what? That anybody who ends up being a priest must have a fatal flaw to begin with? I supposed it doesn't look good, that I showed up back in Superior the day he disappeared.

Rita shifted uncomfortably in her chair. "I didn't put him onto you— exactly. I let it slip that you grew up here and went to Immaculate Heart. Whatever he put together from that, he did on his own." Rita leaned forward in her chair. "Jim, did he ask anything about my father, or Pops?"

"I told him your dad and I were buddies."

"So he did ask. Did you tell him about the drugs? About Pops and my dad not getting along?"

"I might have mentioned it, I honestly don't remember. I got a little rattled when I figured out why he was talking to me."

"Jim, this is important. Is there anything specific, any particular argument my dad and Pops had all the time, over and over? Anything my dad might have told Pops he was going to do, or did do, to prove to Pops that he was a man?"

"You're talking about the 'Nam stuff, Frankie protesting with those college kids all the time."

"Did you protest too? Did you hang out with them?"

"Yeah, I tagged along."

Rita's strategy wasn't getting her where she wanted to go. She could come right out and ask Jim about the ear, but what would it prove if he knew? That he killed Thomas Baker? Or that Rita's father killed Baker and Jim knew it? If Jim *were* guilty, she'd just be alerting him that she was onto him. "You didn't talk to Detective Drake about any of that?" she asked him.

"No, why would I?"

Rita stood up, pacing with frustration. Her respect for Rick's skills went up a few more notches. She struggled to formulate her next question. "I think he, the police, have proof that the two murders are connected. They have physical evidence."

"And it leads back to somebody at Immaculate Heart."

It wasn't a question. Rita's stomach quivered. She fought against the threatening nausea. Pops was right; she should have eaten something.

"You think it's me, don't you?"

She didn't answer.

"Relax Rita. I'm no killer, and I don't know who might be. But I think somebody here did know."

"Who?" Rita sat back down.

"After we talked last time I checked the church archives. Father Bartoelli's record noted a sabbatical, not a transfer. I asked around, to see if anybody recalled him. I said I remembered him fondly and wondered where he might be now. Nobody knew, but one old gal told me he'd had a nervous breakdown."

"A breakdown? Wouldn't everybody have known that?"

"I think she might have been exaggerating a bit, or had built it up in her mind over the years. Bottom line is she overheard a conversation between Father Bartoelli and the Monsignor. She was the church secretary, said she couldn't help hearing through the walls between the two offices."

"Mrs. Johnson?"

"You know her?"

"I know who she is." Rita said.

"Well, I get the feeling she probably did a lot of listening at keyholes. Anyway, she said it was about a year after the Baker boy was killed."

"What did she overhear?" Rita asked.

"Bartoelli was a wreck, *sobbing* is the word she used. Telling the Monsignor he'd prayed until his knees were blistered but his conscience was still heavy. He believed if he wasn't granted the sabbatical, someplace far away from Superior, he'd have to tell what he knew."

"What *did* he know?"

"The old woman couldn't say. Bartoelli and the Monsignor never named it, he just advised the priest that he couldn't break the seal."

"The seal?" Rita dug into her memories. "The seal of the confessional?"

"That'd be the one. Of course, now that sexual abuse by priests is such a scandal, she's positive that's what it was all about. *Some poor boy who told about those awful priests in confession,* she said." He'd softened his voice to imitate her. "Or maybe one of the *troubled priests looking for absolution,* as she put it."

"Troubled. Such a nice way of putting it," Rita said. "Why are you telling me this? You're a priest yourself. Aren't you betraying your brotherhood or something?"

"Maybe. That's up to interpretation, and the way I see it, if a cop thinks I might have something to do with the murder of two boys, I'm going to tell him everything I know that doesn't break any vow I took."

"So you told Drake?" Rita asked.

"I told him there was a rumor that Bartoelli left because of something he knew."

"So *somebody* confessed *something.* That's not much to go on."

"Something bad enough that Bartoelli wanted to tell, but couldn't," Father Jim said, "I'm leaning toward murder. I mean, if it were me, and another priest confessed to molesting children, I know I couldn't break that seal, but I could certainly watch him, bring his questionable actions to the attention of my superiors. I wouldn't feel totally helpless. But something like murder, a deed done once and over? That might make me a little crazy."

"Could Bartoelli have told the Monsignor what the confession was about—if he kept the confessor's identity secret?"

"No, he wouldn't be able to tell the Monsignor any details, only that he was struggling with his vow to keep the seal. The Monsignor would have told him his only course of action would be to encourage the confessor to atone for his sin, and to pray for himself."

"Atone how?"

"Confessing to the proper authorities, turning himself in."

Wouldn't that require the assumption that they were talking about something illegal, not just a sin?"

One side of Father Jim's mouth turned up in lopsided grin. "Like I said, astute. In the context of our conversation, right now, that's what he would have advised. I doubt Father Bartoelli would have been so distraught over a minor infraction of the lesser commandments."

"Was there anything in the archives about where Bartoelli went for the sabbatical?"

"Someplace outside of Chicago, an old Catholic school or monastery. I checked and it closed years ago. It's a retirement community now–for priests and nuns."

"How old was Bartoelli? What's the chance he's still alive?

Jim shook his head. "I don't know. When you're a kid, everybody seems old."

"If he's alive, he could still be in the same place," Rita said. Fatigue was beginning to overwhelm her. She felt like she hadn't slept in days. She couldn't force her brain to work anymore.

"I have to get going, Jim. Thanks for talking to me. I'm sorry if I kept you too late." She stood up and started walking back toward the entryway.

Jim followed. "I hope you find your answers, Rita. I'll pray for you."

"Yeah, thanks." They both stopped at the doorway. "One more question?" she asked.

"Anything."

"Did you go to Vietnam?"

"Yeah, I got caught in the draft in '68, I did one tour. All the crazy stories those protesters told us, about the unjust war, and what soldiers were doing over there." He stopped talking.

Rita held her breath. She saw his eyes gloss over, with tears or excitement, she couldn't be sure. Now would be the time to ask him about souvenir body parts–catch him at a weak moment. She hesitated too long.

"Turned out they weren't lying," he continued, "But they weren't telling it all by half. It was a surreal kind of hell, like being on one long acid trip, a bad one. An inferno of napalm flames, wailing and gnashing of teeth, torture, atrocities–everything you ever read about hell in the Bible. It was the end of the line over there. I didn't understand until then."

"Didn't understand what?" she asked.

"What's one more sin? What's the blood of one more life on your hands, or another one, and another after that, once you're already in hell? I have blood on my hands, Rita, but it isn't Thomas Baker's—or Sean Nolan's."

The hairs on the back of Rita's neck stood up. She wanted to bolt out the door, but there was one more thing she had to ask, one more piece of the puzzle that was her father.

"What about my Dad? I know he was a protester, didn't support the war, but a lot of men didn't. How is it he managed to avoid the draft?"

Jim's pained expression changed. He almost smiled. "Francis Andrew Sullivan was 4-F, unfit for service. He showed me the official letter the day it came. I still remember it like it was yesterday, your father laughing, practically dancing around the room, thinking he'd gotten one over on them."

"Unfit? My father? Why?"

"Psych eval, he didn't pass muster."

"But you did."

Rita slipped through the open door and heard it close behind her. She started down the walkway making it as far as the public sidewalk before turning back around to heave into the bushes.

Crouched over, practically on her hands and knees, Rita began to weep. What on earth was she doing? Why couldn't she ever leave well enough alone? She'd thought she was so smart. Thought *she* was going to solve a case the police hadn't been able to crack in fifty years.

She heard Grandma Abby's voice in her head. *Nothing to do about it now but pull yourself up and carry on.* She stood up and walked back to her car. Even with the top down she'd automatically hit the button to lock the doors. She glanced into the backseat looking for the boogieman Pops had warned about, almost hoping to see him there.

It had been acerbic, self-recrimination, but behind the wheel with the wind reviving her once again, it turned out that throwing up was just what she'd needed. Still, it didn't change the fact that she left the rectory with more questions than answers.

Her father's 4-F classification was a new twist. Soldiers had to be certifiably, bat-shit crazy to get out on a psych evaluation, but just how crazy did one have to be to stay out in the first place? And she didn't appreciate Pops not telling her about her medical history.

When she got home, she walked straight past the kitchen and living room into her bedroom. She undid her jeans, peeling them down past her knees, kicking and stomping them the rest of the way off, leaving them in an inside-out heap on the floor. She maneuvered her bra out from under her t-shirt by unhooking the back and reaching up under the loose cotton garment to slide the straps off her shoulders. She didn't bother to wash her face or brush her teeth. All she wanted was to crawl into bed, fall asleep, and forget the day had ever happened.

She got half her wish. She fell asleep—passed out more likely, but woke up an hour before her alarm went off with all of the questions of the previous day still jumbled in her mind. Her head was pounding and her stomach was growling. She had to pee. She dealt with that first. Then she dissolved a couple of Alka-Seltzers in a glass of water while she waited for her coffee to brew.

Old remedies were still the best. After downing the seltzer and sipping the first cup of strong coffee, her head didn't hurt as much. She found leftover fried chicken in the fridge from the Chicken Spur on Hammond at the bottom of the High Bridge.

She ate it cold, washing it down with more coffee while pondering the odds of having two bridges across the same bay with names that seemed to reference drug culture. Where else but the Twin Ports could you literally cross over the Bong Bridge and return on the High Bridge?

Okay, technically one of them was the Blatnik Bridge, named for former U.S. Congressman John Blatnik, but the official name and dedication didn't come until ten years after the bridge was built. By that time, everybody had been calling it the high bridge for so long the name just stuck. The Bong Bridge was named for local flyboy and WWII Ace, Richard Ira Bong. Same as the veterans' museum where Bong's restored P-38 Lightning was housed.

Rita chased her breakfast with a half bottle of warm Pepsi she'd left sitting on the coffee table, right where she'd dropped her purse and keys the night before. She didn't remember stopping to buy the soda, but the jolt of carbonated, caramel colored, high fructose syrup was the finishing touch she needed. Power breakfast for the busy reporter. She almost felt like a new woman.

It was raining out; she could hear a light patter of drops on the street in the predawn stillness. A southwesterly wind ruffled the sheer curtains at the window; it would likely push the clouds out over the lake before mid-morning. She checked the windowsill to see if the rain had come in through the screen, but it was dry.

Rain before seven, clear skies by eleven. Grandma Abby had taught her that. It would be a perfect morning for a walk if the skies cleared sooner. Since her divorce, Rita found a sense of freedom in being able to come and go any time of day or night without having to explain to somebody where she was going, which was usually nowhere in particular, or why she preferred walking alone—usually to clear her mind.

Curled into the corner of her sofa listening to the sound of the rain, her mind wandered back over the events of the last few days. How ironic was it to be so preoccupied with not one, but two brutal murders right in her own town, and yet never be worried about her own safety, sleeping with her windows open and often walking the streets alone at all hours?

Superior was a big town and a small town all in one. Geographically, it sprawled out on the landscape at the western tip of Lake Superior, yet by population it was barely a city. Violent crime was almost non-existent, or at least less random. When it did happen, it was usually one of two things, substance abuse or domestic violence—most often a combination of the two. Nearly every violent death that occurred in Superior for as long as she could remember had been at the hands of a family member or someone the victim knew well.

Maybe that was why the Baker case stood out. The very lack of evidence said it was random, perpetrated by an unknown, possibly with no connection to the victim at all. Except for the shirt pulled over his head. *Every rule has an exception.*

And now there was Sean Nolan to add to the mix. She was almost certain the two were connected, but what if she was wrong? What if the coincidences between the two were as random as the murders themselves? What if it was copycat? It all hinged on the ear, and whether or not Sean's had been severed too.

Rita knew one thing for sure; Rick wasn't going to tell her what she wanted to know. And after last night, she'd given up any idea she had of coming right out and asking Father Jim if he'd sliced off the Baker kid's ear to frame her father.

She leaned her head down on the arm of the sofa. She didn't spook easily, but Father Jim's soul-baring admission of having blood on his hands gave her the creeps. He had fellow priests to dump that on, why tell her?

She sat up. Was it a veiled threat? Was he warning her to stop digging around?

She picked up her phone and quickly pulled up the paper's website. She clicked on the obituary tab. Just as she feared, she'd already missed Sean Nolan's visitation—it had been held last night.

Damn, why wasn't I thinking?

She knew perfectly well why. Clear thinking departed somewhere after the second shot of slivo and before the tumblers of gin. In her own defense, she'd never planned on going to Sean Nolan's visitation *or* funeral; there was no reason to before Pops dropped his bombshell. Now she was kicking herself for missing the opportunity to do a little reconnaissance. If Sean Nolan *were* missing an ear, those guys at Lenroot's would have a pretty hard time covering it up with makeup.

She sighed. Now it was too late. The casket would be closed for the service. Maybe somebody at the visitation could tell her.

She picked up her phone and called into the editor's desk. The Friday edition was already off the press and on the newsstands. There was nothing urgent on her desk. If push came to shove, technically she could say she was still working on the story.

It was still too early for even her over-worked editor to be in the office. Rita waited through the voice message for the beep. "It's Rita. I won't be in until this afternoon. I've got a funeral." She went back to bed and set her alarm for ten.

XII

When Rita crawled out of bed for the second time that day, the sun was shining, and any evidence of the early morning rain had burned off. Grandma Abby, right again. After showering, dressing in her gray funeral pants and white blouse, and wrapping her wet hair in a loose bun, Rita hurried out the door.

The Immaculate Heart cathedral was the largest church in Superior—of any domination. Its steeple was supposed to be a beacon drawing in spiritual seekers, but to Rita it now seemed to cast a long shadow instead.

The cathedral was one of only four Catholic Churches left in the city. There had been more than a dozen before the faithful started staying away in droves. Most of them had their own schools early on, but one by one the classrooms were scaled back, eliminating high school and then junior high grades. Eventually, all Catholic students were funneled to Immaculate Heart, saving the school for a time, by the grace and good fortune of families who liked the idea of a private education—parochial or not.

The bloom of summer flowers in the landscaped bed reminded Rita of Sister Margaret Ann tending the flowerbeds, inviting the girls of Immaculate Heart to kneel in the dirt beside her. She'd opened their minds to the science of flowers and their eyes to the beauty of spring violets, bright colored tulips, and Sister's favorite, the iris and daisies that bloomed in the summer. Classes might be suspended from June to September, but the call to duty was never silent for an Immaculate Heart student within eyesight of a priest or nun.

Rita looked at the clusters of tall, pale yellow iris blooming atop chartreuse stems with narrow, blade-shaped leaves. She heard Sister Margaret Ann's voice again, as if she were still that nine-year-old girl kneeling in the warm soil beside the wise old nun.

"Isn't it just amazing? From these gnarled, ugly rhizomes the most beautiful blooms will burst forth," she'd explained. "I don't understand when people say the age of miracles has passed. God's miracles unfold around us every day and we can share in the process."

Sister Margaret Ann had given Rita a handful of the rhizomes she'd helped to dig and separate, telling her to plant them in her yard. "Do you see the roots?" she'd asked. "They need to grow deep into the soil, to nourish the plant. But the shoulders have to feel the sun." She pointed to the knobby, rough rhizomes. "Don't plant them too deep in the soil. If you do, they won't bloom," she said.

"What if I do it wrong?" Rita asked.

"Do your best, Rita. If you get it right, you will be rewarded with flowers for years to come," Sister Margaret had answered. "It's one way God teaches us faith and patience." There was always a religious lesson with the nuns.

Rita understood the science, but never quite cultivated the virtues. Patience was tedious. As for faith, Rita put hers in concrete facts.

Rita wheeled her little car around the corner and into the parking lot. The expanse of blacktop hadn't always been there. Immaculate Heart's numbers increased with each closing of another parish. People complained about having to park blocks away.

"So they paved paradise and put up a parking lot," Rita sang out loud, to nobody but herself. Aunt Sue had been a big influence in Rita's musical repertoire.

Rita recalled the wide expanse of soft, plush grass she and the other Immaculate Heart students played on during recess beginning each fall semester. They'd pile radiant yellow, orange, and red leaves into huge mounds, scattering them again when they leapt into the pile. Later in the year they'd build winter snow forts, and make snow men and snow angels. In the spring, when the air was redolent with the heady scent of lilacs bursting open into plump, purple cones, the whole student body would seem to grow absolutely giddy with spring fever and the anticipation of summer vacation.

She remembered the rows of peonies beneath the church windows. First the buds, tight little balls of green with tell-tale pink margins, crawling with swarms of black ants, then followed by blooms of fringed petals so profuse the weight of them caused the flower heads to bow down. According to Sister Margaret Ann, they did it in reverent humility, the showiest of flowers in the garden humbling themselves before their creator.

Rita marveled at how interwoven Immaculate Heart was in the memories of her early life, warp and weft. No wonder she could never completely untangle herself from its influence.

It hadn't been bad, really. In fact, her time there was almost idyllic. What she would give now to go back to the blessing of those long, lazy summer days in the church yard, setting out impromptu picnics on blankets spread beneath the branches of the oak and maple trees—a natural canopy of shade. Lying on the ground in the cool shadows, eating peanut butter and jelly sandwiches with her best friends Betsy and Michelle, gazing up at the clouds and dreaming of their futures.

The peonies would be blooming just about this time of year, Rita thought. When she closed her eyes she could smell the heavenly fragrance, more intoxicating even than lilacs. How many times had she dreamed of carrying a wedding bouquet of lilacs and peonies? When the time came, all the florists just smiled politely and told her they couldn't secure fresh blooms of each at the same time, it was an impossible pairing. She should have taken that as a sign.

Rita had taken the iris roots Sister Margaret Ann gave her all those years ago, doing as she'd been told. Her half-dozen irises came up year after year, multiplying into several dozen in Grandma Abby's flowerbed, eventually blooming every year just as Sister had promised.

When Rita and Mark purchased their first home, Rita felt compelled to take some of the irises from Grandma Abby's to plant in her own yard. And when she left there, she divided those, planting her half beneath the window of the apartment she lived in now. There was no going back to that innocent childhood she had grown out of, but she'd managed to take a small piece of it with her, just the same.

Rita got out of her little bug, shutting the door on her car and her memories behind her.

The church was packed. She doubted everybody cramming into the cathedral had a personal connection to Sean or his family. She bet half of them were there out of curiosity, getting grist for the conversation mill. Sean Nolan was the chatter all over social media, at every cafe and kitchen table, in every bar, and around every coffee machine in every break room in town.

Rick was there, along with a few other cops out of uniform. They were watching the crowd, the same as Rita was, but she wasn't looking for a killer. Not today, anyhow.

Rita was looking for somebody who would talk to her. Not the kind who wanted their name in the paper—those were a dime a dozen, eager to tell her how they knew Sean or his family, that he was a great kid and what a terrible tragedy this was. She stood at the rear of the packed church, watching the backs of mourners' heads, looking for tells that might set one apart from all the others.

His parents sat in the front pew on the right side, clinging to each other in their desperate grief. His mother wept openly. His father's broad shoulders were hunched and shaking with his own tears, no crying out that Rita could hear. The rest of the pew was likely family, maybe close friends—adults and children. More of the same sat in the pews to the left of the aisle.

Starting several pews back, on both sides, were the kids, rows of them. They couldn't all be Sean's friends, and that's who Rita wanted to talk to. A lot of the boys fidgeted, uncomfortable with their own emotions. All the girls seemed to be crying, some of them more openly than others.

When the service was over, the mourners filed out of church to their cars. Rita stayed on the church steps, watching the cars leave the lot one by one to take their places in the long procession that would wind through town to Tower Avenue, out to South End and on to Calvary Cemetery. Once Sean was in his grave, they'd turn around and come back to the church for the requisite luncheon.

A few drivers waited to leave until the cavalcade heading for the cemetery cleared the parking lot. Some would come back, after a drink or three at one of the nearby bars on East 5th Street—Dodgies, The Office, or Pudge's. Rita considered following them. But, back at the visitation, a little alcohol would loosen tongues, too. It wouldn't be hard to lead a conversation there, find out if the casket had been open or closed, elicit a few comments about Sean's appearance.

Or maybe not. Post-funeral conversation usually didn't get to the subject of what had brought them all there until they were all several drinks in.

Eventually, Rita made her way back inside the church and headed downstairs to the parish hall basement. She'd try her luck with the other stragglers avoiding the actual burial. There was a particular young girl who'd seemed removed, or maybe numbed, during the service. Rita was sure she saw her heading down into the parish hall.

About halfway down the stairwell opened to a familiar sight, a sea of banquet tables covered in white paper and dotted with dollar store flower arrangements. It made Rita dizzy. She gripped the stair railing and looked down at her feet, fighting the sudden panic that threatened to overwhelm her. She wondered if her anxiety caused the vertigo, or the other way around. Taking a deep breath, she steadied herself and descended the last of the steps.

Rita lingered first at the coffee service table, then tried sitting in a central location to eavesdrop on nearby mourners. Nothing. She moved aimlessly around the perimeter. Still nothing; she hadn't overheard a single thing about the visitation or Sean's appearance—not one mention of how peaceful he looked, or how natural. Maybe his casket *had* been closed.

She was ready to give up and admit the whole thing had been a waste of time when she spotted the young girl she'd watched during the funeral slipping out of the restroom door up the steps to the side entrance. She looked back over her shoulder before ducking out the door. Rita decided to follow her.

Outside she caught a glimpse of the girl turning the corner around the back of the rectory. Rita walked quietly to the end of the building and waited. First she heard the click of a lighter, and then caught a distinct whiff of cigarette smoke.

Perfect. She'd bum a cigarette, see if she could get the girl to talk. Warm her up a little and then toss in something about feeling bad she'd missed the visitation the night before. She relaxed her arms at her side, shaking her hands to dispel the nervous energy she felt, then strolled casually around the corner.

The girl looked up quickly, surprised by Rita's sudden appearance. She'd been crying, here, where nobody could see. A few strands of her long hair stuck to her wet cheeks. She dropped her left hand down to her side, trying to hide the cigarette from Rita.

"I saw you leaving the parish hall. Figured you might be coming out for a smoke."

"Yeah." The girl looked at Rita for a second, her plucked eyebrows raised a little, then took a drag on her cigarette and turned away. It was going to be challenge to overcome the weird factor of some total stranger of a middle-aged woman chatting her up, but Rita was used to playing that role.

She filled the awkward quiet between them with a few words. "I'm trying to quit. Not doing a very good job of it."

The girl remained silent.

"Think maybe you'd loan me a cigarette?" The girl handed Rita her lit one in silent response. Well, it was something, anyhow.

"Thanks," Rita said, taking a long puff without inhaling the smoke into her lungs. She held it in her mouth for a bit before blowing it out. It still made her cough. "It's been a while," she said, taking one more fake drag before passing the cigarette back.

The girl still wasn't talking. Rita used the silence to take in the details. She had honey blonde hair shot through with strands the color of pale wheat. Her brown eyes and medium skin tone suggested it was an expensive salon job. Her black jeans were meant to look well worn with faded creases in strategic zones, but they were new. The flip-flops she was wearing revealed a perfect French pedicure. She brought her cigarette up to her mouth to take another puff, but instead her breath caught in an involuntary sob, the kind that comes after crying hard.

In the bathroom? Rita thought. *And she couldn't stop, so she ducked outside.*

Yet she'd managed to hold it together through the service, her head never once bowing in grief, her shoulders steady. Rita looked at the rings on her pinky and middle finger, narrow bands of bright gold. The sunlight bounced of the bracelet on her wrist, a circle of what Rita was sure must be diamonds. The girl came from money and plenty of it, a level of class that accepted nothing less than public composure. *Save your tears for the pillow.*

Sean's father drove truck, his mother was a CNA—solid middle class. This girl was way out of the boy's social league, but she was clearly broken up by his death. She could be a relative, but Rita didn't think so. She made one more attempt to gain her confidence.

"You were close, weren't you?" Rita asked in a soft voice.

The girl chewed on her bottom lip trying not to cry, but the tears slid down her cheeks. Rita reached into her purse for a Kleenex and handed it to the girl.

"Thanks," she said, taking the tissue.

"You're welcome. My name's Rita, by the way."

The girl just nodded while she dabbed at her eyes.

Rita would just have to ask, then. "And you are?"

"Oh, sorry. I'm Kristy."

"Are you here with somebody, Kristy?" She'd seen a woman with identical blonde hair sitting in the pew next to the girl.

"My mother. She *insisted* on coming with me."

"Parents worry," Rita said. "Where is she now?"

"The cemetery. I told her I didn't want to go," The girl's tears started up again, falling in a continuous stream. She squeezed her eyes shut trying to stop them.

"And she left you here?"

"I just wanted to leave, not go to the cemetery or come back here." Kristy paused, shooting another quick look at Rita. This was a little weird, Rita had to admit, getting an emotionally distraught young girl to just open up to her like this. She was just about to offer some thanks for the drag and walk away when the girl continued.

"My mom said it would be rude to leave now and I should have thought of all this before insisting on coming to the funeral. She doesn't understand." Kristy choked down another deep sob. "I started crying in the bathroom and she told me to stay there until I could get myself under control. She thinks I'm such a child." She took another drag off the cigarette. "She hasn't got a clue."

Blaming her mother for treating her like a baby and complaining at having to act like an adult practically in the same breath. Rita wondered if Kristy was younger than she'd first thought. "Were you and Sean classmates?"

"Yeah. My mother thinks that's why I'm here too, like it couldn't be anything more than that."

"Is it more than that?" Of course it was. Kristy didn't want her mother to know that—and at the same time, did.

"My parents won't let me date until I'm sixteen. They're so clueless, like just saying so was going to stop me."

Rita was beginning to understand Kristy. Sean was dead, and nobody who counted knew that she was his girlfriend.

"So you were his girlfriend."

"We never even had a real date, and now it's too late." Kristy's words caught in another deep, hiccoughing sob. She dropped her cigarette and crushed it out on the grass. She lifted her head, holding Rita's gaze much longer than the first few furtive glances she'd taken. Her look that asked for so much. "You got kids?"

Rita shook her head. "Nope." She felt a sudden urge to reach out and hug the girl but didn't. The feeling surprised her, but she didn't think she'd ever seen a child who needed the comfort of her mother's arms more than this broken-hearted girl standing in front of her.

Kristy turned away and put her back up against the building, crossing her arms. She leaned her head against the wall. "My mom doesn't have a clue," she said again.

"What about Sean's mom? I mean, does she know about you? Did she know you were Sean's girlfriend?

She smiled, briefly, hearing the words out loud, then the moment passed as quickly as it came. "No. I never met her. Never even saw her before last night."

"You were at the visitation?" *Jackpot!*

"Yeah. A few of my friends came by and we told my mother we were going out for pizza. It was weird, seeing him like that. It looked like him, but it didn't—something was missing."

Rita's heart skipped a beat. "Missing? What do you mean?"

"I don't know; it's hard to explain. It was like looking at a doll, or a wax dummy in one of those museums, I guess. I mean I've never really been to one, but that's what I thought of when I saw him."

Rita forced a chuckle. "Oh, you had me wondering for a minute. I thought you meant something was actually missing, like an injury or from being in the water." She added the water part for good measure. She knew Sean hadn't been there long enough for decomposition.

"You mean like a *part* of him? Gross." She uncrossed her arms and turned back towards Rita. "Why would you think something like that? It's weird."

"Yeah, sorry. I probably watch too many of those CSI shows on television." There was a pause in the conversation, but Kristy didn't seem in a hurry to leave. "It's the heavy makeup they use."

"Yeah, I guess."

That was it then; Rita knew Kristy couldn't tell her what she wanted to know. "Your mom will be back soon."

"Yeah." Kristy leaned back against the building and tilted her face toward the sun again. "I should have gone, you know?"

"To the cemetery?"

"I just knew I couldn't keep it together a minute longer, and my mother would have a fit if I was *hysterical* in public."

She stopped talking, but Rita sensed she wasn't done yet. "I just wish she knew, I wish she'd be okay with it so I could tell her how I feel."

"I remember a boy I went to school with," she said. "I had a huge crush on him, used to find excuses to show up wherever he was, you know?"

"I gotta say, that's sounds kind of lame. Sort of sweet, but lame."

"Yeah, it was. He never did notice me, not the way I wanted him to, not the way Sean noticed you."

"He was just so easy to talk to, you know? When he wasn't with his stupid friends. He showed off too much around them. Talked big, liked to brag a lot, but that's not how he was with me."

"Well, just so you know, they never seem to outgrow that. They all have to brag about something. Harmless, I guess, as long as it's not about other girls."

"Yeah." Kristy smiled a little again. "He didn't do that. He just wasn't like that, wanting to hook up with any girl that would lie down for him."

"A gentleman," Rita said. "And so early in the game."

"That's why he didn't want me hanging around when he was with his friends. He didn't want them to think it was that way with us."

Rita spent about two seconds thinking that over. Wouldn't a guy who had real feelings show it in public, whatever his friends thought be damned? But what did she know? Maybe that's not how it worked anymore. She hadn't had a real date in how many years? And these were kids, just starting to figure it all out. Besides, who was she to talk? Her arrangement with Rick wasn't any better, always keeping in the shadows, out of public view. Still, it ticked her radar. "So what did Sean brag about then?" she asked.

"The car his dad was fixing up for him to drive as soon as he got his license, how he did whatever he wanted at home, had the run of the place with his dad on the road and his mom working, how he could sit right in his own living room and have a beer, or a whole six-pack if he wanted to."

Rita could see what attracted Kristy to Sean. Compared to the tight control her parents kept, he was waving a big orange carrot of freedom in front of her.

"It's not like he did, though. He wasn't like that."

It was the second time she said the same thing and the second time Rita's suspicions piqued. She nodded. "Got it."

Kristy stood there for a while. A half-smile moved onto her mouth and right back off again. She had something she wanted to say. Rita knew that look. "Is there something else you wanted to tell me?" she said, leaning in a little with a long-practiced *tell me the story* look on her face.

"Hmmmm." Kristy half-smiled again, shaking her head a little. "It's just that I'm telling you . . . *Rita*, right? telling you things and you just walked up here wanting a drag a few minutes ago."

Rita made a little noise like she understood, like this was weird, yes, but no big deal, really.

"Well, whatever. Anyhow, he never stopped bragging about that stupid knife he kept flashing around. He told everybody he found it in the tool shed." She pointed to the small building next to the garage off the back of the parking lot. "That one right there."

Rita turned to look at the building, hoping she'd been quick enough to hide her surprise. Did she really just hear what she thought she heard? She took a breath to calm herself before turning back to Kristy. "A knife he found in the garden shed? Probably just something the gardener uses to dig out weeds. What's to brag about?"

"He told his buddies it belonged to that kid whose name is on the holy water fountain inside the church. It's some urban legend or something–he disappeared and they found him stabbed and drained of blood, but they never found the weapon."

Wow, those facts couldn't be any more convoluted. Where did they get this stuff? "And you're sure he found it in that shed?"

"That's what he told everybody."

"And he didn't–nobody thought they should tell the police?"

"Sean said if it was the one that was used to kill that kid, it had some kind of power in it. I don't know, some weird shit he gets . . . got from reading science fiction. Besides, it was just a kid's folding knife. He probably lost it in that shed doing yard work–like Sean was doing."

She had a point. Anybody could have lost a knife there. Or maybe it wasn't even lost. It could have been there for a reason. "Did he say how he knew it was Thomas Baker's?"

Kristy looked at her, clearly not understanding.

"The boy on the holy water fountain," Rita said.

"His initials were carved in the handle. That's what Sean said anyway. I never saw the thing close. Didn't really care."

How was it possible this girl never considered, even for a moment, that the knife *might* be very important in the larger scheme of things?

Because she's a teenager, she isn't concerned with anything beyond the tip of her own nose. That's how. It was an unfair thought, but at this point Rita was beginning to wonder if the girl had any critical thinking skills to speak of.

"I'm going to head back inside." Kristy said. "I don't want my mom to come looking for me. She'll know for sure I came out to smoke. She's such a hypocrite; smokes like a fiend herself, but never where anybody might see her doing it."

"You should maybe cut her some slack. I'm sure she just wants what's best for you, doesn't want you to get hooked, like her." Rita expected an eye roll. She was surprised when it didn't happen. "I'm real sorry about Sean," she said.

"Yeah, thanks," Kristy said.

Rita thought she might jump out of her skin, trying not to break out in a dead run for her car. Inside with the door closed behind her, she dumped her purse out on the passenger seat and snatched her phone. She couldn't connect to Rick's number fast enough.

"Detective Drake." He answered after only one ring.

"Where are you? Did you go to the cemetery?"

"I did. I just got back to my office. I see you were at the funeral. I'm surprised you didn't come nosing around the grave site. Don't you think the killer would want to see that, too?"

"I wasn't looking for the killer, I was trying to find out. . . Never mind, it doesn't matter what I was doing. I think I found something important."

"What?"

"I don't want to tell you on the phone."

"Come on, Rita, I'm tired. It's been a long day already, and the girls and I are leaving to go see Jane later this afternoon."

Shit. That trip just got cancelled. Rita didn't like to interfere with his obligations to Jane. She wasn't jealous and she didn't want it coming off that way. Rick had been up front with her from the beginning; he wasn't divorcing his wife. At least not anytime soon. His insurance was the only thing covering Jane's care while they waited for a settlement. If he divorced her, she'd be moved out of Serenity House into some over-crowded and under-staffed state or county facility. Beside that, it was still too soon for the girls to think about their father moving on.

"I just talked to a girl who said Sean Nolan was bragging about finding a certain knife the SPD has been wanting to get their hands on for the last fifty years."

"What? Who? Where are you?"

"I'm still at the church."

"Is the girl there?"

"Yes, she's with her mother. They're waiting for the mourners to come back from the cemetery. They're hanging around for the funeral meatballs and cheesy potatoes."

"Keep them there."

Rita wasn't used to being on the receiving end of his barked orders. "What? How am I supposed to do that?"

"Do whatever you have to, just keep her at that church until I get there."

Rita made her way back into the parish hall. *Great. I'll just tell them I'm a pathetic loser here by myself and ask if I can sit with them.*

It wasn't hard to spot the pair. Kristy's mother had the same perfect shade of blonde hair, shoulder length, the kind of precisely cut locks that fall in perfect layers with a quick toss of her head. She wore a crisp, white linen top over well-fitted black Capri pants, and nude colored, leather flats that nearly disappeared against her ever-so-subtle faux tan. If money could walk, Rita was watching it move through the buffet line.

Rick couldn't get there soon enough to suit her. *God, please let all the lights be green.*

XIII

Rita queued into line but kept letting people go ahead of her, explaining that she was waiting for somebody. When Rick arrived, she directed him to Kristy with her eyes. She mouthed the word *blonde* and moved her hand up and down in the air by her head, gesturing *long hair*. Once he'd zeroed in on his subject, she left her place in line. She made the stairs by the time he approached the unsuspecting mother and daughter, but it wasn't soon enough. She glanced back and caught Kristy's searing glare at her. *So much for a beautiful new inter-generational friendship.*

Rita didn't like being a snitch, but she had bigger things than her ethics on her mind. She had to talk to Pops. He was never going to believe what Kristy told her about the knife. She sped to his apartment, taking the stairs two at a time once she was in the building. She wasn't about to wait for the elevator.

She rang Pops's doorbell, leaving the button pushed down longer than necessary, willing her summons to bring him to the door faster. She stood close, almost pressing herself against the solid surface of the door. "Come *on* Pops, be here," she whispered.

No answer. She stepped back and leaned her shoulder against the doorjamb. Would Pops have his cell phone with him? He didn't like using it, even though she'd gotten him the big button, no-frills model and showed him how easy it was to operate. "In case you need it, Pops," she'd cajoled him. "You know, if you have car trouble, or need anything—or maybe just want me to meet you for lunch when you're out and about." Pops grumbled, but he accepted the phone.

Rita pressed the speed dial for his number. "Pick up, pick up," she whispered. To her surprise, he answered before the call transferred to voice mail. "Pops, where are you?"

"I'm on the golf course with Stan. We're just finishing up the ninth hole and then we're heading into the clubhouse for a beverage." Beverage was code for beer; he was so funny sometimes with all of his euphemisms.

"I need to talk to you, right away."

"Meet us at the clubhouse. Did you have lunch yet? They make a decent burger here."

"No, not the clubhouse. Someplace we won't be overheard. Meet me at the park across from the gas station in South End. You know the one."

"Jack's Standard?

"Yes, that one, but they changed the name. Calumet now, same as the refinery."

"Can't you just come here?"

"No, Pops."

"I suppose we could go to 58th Street Diner. They have real malts there," he said.

"Pops, no. I'll be in the park. Just meet me there."

"Rita, what's going on? You're talking crazy."

"You're not going to think it's crazy when you hear what I have to tell you. Just meet me. I'll be there in ten minutes."

"Okay, we'll see you there."

Rita sped down Tower Avenue, not that she stood out from the rest of the drivers; the average speed after clearing the last traffic light at North 37th Street was at least ten miles over the limit. At 58th Street she turned left and pulled the bug up alongside the diner.

The park was empty. No mothers with strollers, no kids on the swings or the climbing bars. That wasn't unusual. She never saw kids in the city parks anymore. She went into the diner and stood at the counter near the cash register. The waitress hustled over. "Hi, what can I do for you?"

"Hi." Rita forced herself to respond with the same cheery tone. "No menu. I just want a couple of malts to go, please."

"Sure thing, hon. What flavor?"

"Both vanilla—malts, not shakes. And can you divide that into three cups?"

"No problem."

The woman was close to Rita's age, but Rita didn't recognize her, not that it mattered. It was just a one-high-school small-town habit, thinking she should know everybody remotely close to her own age.

The waitress made quick work of filling two steel blender cups and snapping them into place on the quad-station machine that had probably been there since the 50s. Rita talked above the loud whir of the motor spinning its slender steel agitators. "Do you have chocolate syrup?"

"I do. Change your mind?"

"No, not really. But when you pour them into the cups, give one a good squirt of chocolate, if you would."

"Not a problem."

"Thanks."

Rita calculated the price for the malts while the woman finished up. She put a ten-dollar bill on the counter, watching the waitress divvy out the malts in three equal portions, and then snap the lids onto each clear cup. She put them in a brown bag, dropped in three straws and a bunch of napkins.

"Keep the change," Rita said, pushing the bill toward the waitress.

"Thanks. You have a good day, now."

She saw Uncle Stan's El Camino parked on the street. Elky was the love of his life. He bought her when he was just eighteen, home on leave between tours. He sent his payment every month while he was overseas and Elky waited in his parent's East End garage. By the time he came home, she was paid for in full.

If Rita ever wondered whether or not OCD ran in her father's family, Elky was the proof. When the Camino was Stan's only means of transportation he'd washed it weekly, with quick rinses from the hose in between. He kept it shined with a coat of hand-rubbed wax year round. As soon as he could afford two cars on his railroad switchman's wages, Elky became a classic car-in-waiting, taken out on the road only in the summer months, tucked away in his garage, safe from the road salt that would corrode her body. Now she was kept in a heated storage unit, from high noon on Labor Day until high noon on Memorial Day—you could set your clock by it.

Rita hurried across the street. Pops and Stan were sitting on a bench under a shade tree, waiting for her. Rita handed them each a cup from the bag. "I got us a treat," she said.

"Real malts?" Pops asked." He never said malt without first saying real. It was like one word for him.

"Of course," Rita answered.

Both men reached eagerly for the cups. Grandma Abby had a malt machine that Pops had given her—a Hamilton Beach just like the one in the diner, except a single cup model he bought off a guy going out of business. Rita remembered her grandmother making the cool treats on hot summer nights after dinner, always dividing it into three glasses, and always saying,

A little bit for everybody, not too much for anybody. She and Rita would add Hershey's syrup to theirs, stirring it in the glass.

"I got you both vanilla," Rita said. "I hope that's okay with you, Uncle Stan."

"Never look a gift horse in the mouth," he said, "but you should try their strawberry sometime."

"Okay Rita, what's up?" Pops asked her. "What's so bad that you need to soften me up first?"

"It's not bad, Pops. In fact, I think it could be pretty good." She sat down between the two men, who'd made room for her on the bench. She leaned forward, almost teetering on the front edge, turning slightly toward Pops.

"I just came from Sean Nolan's funeral." She watched his smile turn into a frown.

"What were you doing there?" Pops asked.

For the first time since Kristy lobbed that hand grenade in the churchyard, Rita realized she'd never gotten the information she'd gone there for. "I was trying to find somebody who might tell me if his casket was opened or closed at the visitation last night."

"Why?" Stan asked between sips of his malt.

"Because I figured somebody might notice if he was missing an ear."

"Oh, for the love of Pete. They'd give him a wax one, Rita." Pops said.

"Well, I think it would be easy to tell if it wasn't real. Somebody might have noticed. I'd notice."

"No, you wouldn't." Pops said.

"I think I would." She really didn't want to argue with him now, but there was still one bone she had to pick. May as well get it over with. "Tell me something Pops. Why haven't you gone to the station, called in a favor, sweet-talked some rookie? Why haven't you asked to see Sean Nolan's file? Wouldn't it tell you everything you need to know?"

"Yes. And maybe something I don't want to know."

Rita nudged her sunglasses up and rubbed her eyes in one continuous motion, letting the frames fall back into place when she was done.

"Fine, whatever. It doesn't matter, Pops, because I found out something else, something very important. I followed Sean Nolan's girlfriend out to the back of the church where she was sneaking a smoke. She told me that Sean found a knife in the tool shed at the rectory—the same one the police have been looking for these last fifty years." She had Pops's full attention now.

"In the rectory tool shed?" Uncle Stan asked.

"A girlfriend?" Pops asked. "They're fifteen, what does that mean at fifteen?"

"A lot more than it did when you were a kid, or when I was for that matter." Rita said. "But so what? Did you hear what I said?"

"How do you know this girl was Nolan's girlfriend? Seems pretty suspicious, or a little too lucky, if you ask me."

"Why? If he had a girlfriend, she'd certainly be at his funeral. I was there, looking for somebody who might know him well, somebody I might be able to chat up and get some information. I found her."

"Stumbled on her, sounds like." Pops was shaking his head. "That kind of luck doesn't happen often."

"Pops. The knife. This is about the knife."

"I know. I'm getting there. Nolan found a knife."

Stan interrupted. "How does she know that it's *the* knife?" he asked.

"Sean was bragging about it, to her and to his friends. It had Thomas Baker's initials on it."

"And he said he found it in the shed? After all these years? Just lying there in plain sight? Sounds fishy if you ask me." Stan took a long suck on his straw, rattling the dregs of the malt at the bottom of his cup until he was satisfied he'd gotten every last drop. "I mean, if it was me, I'd toss it off a bridge. They'd never find it in Lake Superior. What do you think, Dave?"

"How long did Sean have this knife?" Pops asked.

"I don't know. I didn't ask her that."

"Where exactly in the shed did he find it?"

"I didn't ask that either."

Pops raised his bushy eyebrows. "Your first real clue and you forget to ask the important questions. Who else knew about the knife, beside this girl and Sean's friends that he bragged to? Why didn't he turn it in if he knew what it was, that it was part of an unsolved case?"

"Well, for one thing, they have all the facts wrong. They think the knife was the murder weapon and that his body was completely drained of blood, as in vampires."

"Vampires wouldn't need a knife to do that. Don't these kids read anymore?" Stan asked.

Rita just looked at him. "Who cares? Their little urban legend made the knife a coveted item. Sean wasn't about to give that up."

"Weapons always make boys feel powerful," Stan said. "But the weapon doesn't give you power, you give the weapon power. It was the hardest thing we had to teach the grunts in basic."

"The point is, he found it in the tool shed at the rectory–one more connection to Immaculate Heart," Rita said. "Can you believe it? Right there in the tool shed, this whole time."

"It is pretty hard to believe," Pops said. "Fifty years is a long time. Somebody could have put it there recently."

"The killer?" Stan asked. "That wouldn't make any sense. Not after all these years of getting away with murder."

"He's right, Pops. That makes no sense."

"Who was the maintenance man back then?" Stan asked. "Seems like the cops should be talking to him."

"John something. It escapes me now." Pops said. "He wouldn't have had anything to do with this. Good family man, as I remember. Worked the night shift at the refinery and took the maintenance job at church to defray his kids' tuition–had a whole slew of them all going to The Heart."

"The refinery?" Rita asked.

Stan looked up from the empty malt cup he was holding between his knees. "Oh sure, sure. Didn't they find that kid on along the refinery road? I mean, I don't remember it so much–I was still overseas then, but that was it, wasn't it?"

"That's where they found him, but it doesn't mean anything." Pops said.

"It doesn't exactly rule him out, Pops," Rita said.

"You're getting caught up in the minutia, Rita. It trips you up. John was questioned along with everybody else working at Immaculate Heart when the Baker kid was killed. He didn't seem fool enough to hide a knife from a crime he'd committed in a tool shed on church property. If he was looking for places to hide it, there'd be a hundred better choices out at the refinery."

"Like at the bottom of a crude oil tank," Stan said.

"Where is it now?" Pops asked.

"I don't know. I called Rick and told him what the girl said. He was at the church talking to her when I left. They'll probably search Sean's house, go through his things. Obviously he didn't have it on him when he died."

"They won't find it," Pops said.

"Why? What makes you think that?"

"Don't you see? It's the knife that connects the two boys, not the church. It's the motive for Sean's death. Somebody besides his girlfriend and his buddies knew he found it, knew *where* he found it, and had to make sure nobody else would ever find out, because that was the scene of the crime."

"The tool shed?" Rita asked.

"So then it *was* a priest," Stan said.

"Jim," Rita offered. "They were in that shed for the same reason Sean's girlfriend snuck out behind the church this morning. I'd bet my life on it."

"A cigarette?" Stan asked.

"No, more like a joint. Or, maybe even a quick hit of speed, some uppers or downers before mass. Something goes wrong, the Baker kid hits his head, Jim panics." Rita said.

"Are you two having fun chasing your tails?" Pops asked. "This drug angle isn't anything I didn't already think of. It could have happened that way, but it also could've been Frankie in that shed, *if* that's where it all went down. Nothing has changed that."

"Jim told me something last night, about Father Bartoelli," Rita said.

"I remember Father Bartoelli," Stan said. "He was young, around my age. Everybody liked him."

"That's odd. Jim thought he was older," Rita said.

"He acted your age," Pops said to Stan. "Organizing youth rallies for peace and pushing those guitar masses, trying to get those hippies to come to church." Pops said.

"Anyway, he wasn't transferred to another church," Rita said. "He took a sabbatical. The rumor at the time was that he was having a crisis of faith. The church secretary, I think the same woman you helped with the bookkeeping, Pops. She overheard a conversation with the monsignor about not breaking the seal."

"A confession?" Pops asked. "Of murder?"

"According to Jim if they were talking about the seal, it was a confession, but to murder? Nobody but Father Bartoelli would have known that."

"But it was after the Baker boy was killed? You're sure of that?" Pops asked.

"Within the year, according to what Jim told me."

"Still, nobody can prove it, right? Unless Father Bartoelli spills the beans," Stan said. "Is he even still alive?"

"Rita, why didn't you tell me about this confession earlier?" Pops asked.

"Jim just told me last night." She saw the growing excitement reflected in her grandfather's expression. He looked positively giddy.

"It wasn't Frankie. It couldn't have been. Frankie never remembered a thing when he came home that morning." Pops looked at Stan. "Remember, Stan? I told you he didn't remember anything, not where he was the night before, or that morning. Nothing. What would he confess to if he didn't remember?"

"So it was Father Jim? He framed his own best friend?" Stan asked.

"What else did Jim say to you, Rita?" Pops asked.

"He did say something odd about being in Vietnam, how it was like being in hell, that it felt like the end."

"The end of what?" Pops asked.

"Of life, I guess. He said after a while, it didn't matter how much blood he had on his hands, what's one more when you're already in hell."

"Sounds about right to me," Stan said. "It was bad business over there."

"But you went back," Rita said. "After the first time you went for another tour."

"They made me an offer I couldn't refuse." He smiled at her. "Promoted me, put me in a Seal team. It seemed like a better plan than just sitting around back home."

Rita remembered filing the story about the young Iraqi veteran in Superior, who killed his girlfriend and then turned his weapon on himself. All of his friends, down to the last one, said it was the stress of coming back and trying to live a normal life.

The incident had haunted her for weeks, and then angered her. She tried to do a story, interview the VA about failing to identify at-risk veterans. Nobody would talk to her. "But we still keep sending our boys off to war, don't we?" she said. "Some things will never make sense."

The three sat on the bench in silence until Pops spoke. "Well, I'm damn sure going to try to make some sense of this. Stan, take me home. I want to get my own car."

"Where are you going Pops? I'll take you."

"No. I'm going to talk to Father Jim, and I don't want you with me."

"No way, Pops. If he's guilty, he could be dangerous."

"Where did you leave that common sense last night?" he asked her.

"I–" She felt the same disappointment she always felt when she let Pops down. "It's dangerous for you, too, Pops."

"I'm eighty-six years old; my wife is gone. My only son is gone and I've spent the last fifty years thinking that he was responsible for somebody else's death. I also spent a good portion of that time resenting your grandmother because her memories of him were untainted. God rest her soul, she had enough of her own pain to deal with and I was wishing more on her."

"Pops, you were good to Grandma Abby. You loved her and she loved you."

He was bent over with his elbows on his thighs, wringing his clasped hands. "I let her think I didn't love our son. I never talked about him," He looked down at his hands. "I couldn't listen to her when she wanted to talk about him. I couldn't bear her grief on top of the load of guilt I was carrying for treating him so badly. I was selfish."

She wanted to comfort him, wanted to put her hand on his shoulder. She'd tried that when Grandma Abby died and he'd pushed it away. "Grandma understood, Pops. She knew you didn't talk about him because it hurt too much."

"He was just getting his life straightened around, you know? After you were born? His little Rita; you were his reason for waking up every day. He beamed every time he looked at you."

"Pops, don't."

"I should have told you all the stories about him growing up. About how much he loved your grandmother's cherry pie, and how he would shiver until his lips turned blue, but wouldn't come out of the water down on Wisconsin Point. And all the stray pets he dragged home."

"Aunt Sue told me. She told me all the stories, Pops."

"It should have been me. I should have talked about your father every day."

"It's okay, Pops. It's okay." Rita stood up. She couldn't hug him. It wasn't that he was cold, or didn't love her. He was just too proud; he could never let himself look weak to the people who counted on him. "I'll take you home," she said. "Then I'll call Rick to see if he has any information about the knife."

XIV

Rita stayed with Pops at his apartment until she had his word that he wouldn't confront Father Jim alone. She'd warmed up the rest of Stan's sarma for their supper. Pops was happy she got to share some with him after all.

She still hadn't received a call back from Rick after texting him. "Pops, I don't think Detective Drake is going to call back tonight. I should go home. You're staying in, right?"

"I promised you."

"Okay. I'll call you tomorrow. You going to be all right?"

"I'm just going to watch a little TV, the old shows on that cable channel. Like me, old and irrelevant," he grumbled.

Ever since Grandma Abby passed, Pops did his best to put on a good face for Rita. Everything was either okay, or going to get better–not to worry. But she knew that wasn't always how he felt. She'd found little notes laying around, things he wrote to Grandma Abby about how much he missed her and Frankie, how the evenings were the loneliest, and how he'd bet there were better things to do up in heaven than watch old reruns until he could go to bed without it being too early.

"I could stay," she said.

"Don't be silly. I'm just going to turn the TV on and I'll probably fall asleep right in my chair before I'm half-way through the first Perry Mason rerun. Drive carefully."

"I always do, Pops. I was taught by the best."

Rita felt limp as wilted lettuce when she finally pulled away from the curb in front of his building. She bypassed the turn that would take her home, though, and headed for the waterfront and Barker's Island. There, she turned left into the nearly empty parking lot, more than an acre of blacktop designed to accommodate the crowds of tourists that never did materialize after the last big redevelopment.

It was a man-made sandbar that almost seemed cursed. Three times in the city's long history it had been positioned as a recreation area, and three times all the money put into development would have done as much good as if they'd thrown it into the bay.

All but two of the businesses at the north end of the island were defunct now, the modern buildings leased to research facilities studying Lake Superior habitat. The mini golf course hung on in the shadow of the Whaleback Ship Museum, both managing to draw enough tourist dollars to make it through each summer.

She pulled her bug into the parking space closest to the ship. Rita had worked as a tour guide on the Meteor for two summers when she was in high school. The story of Captain McDougall and his whaleback ships was fascinating, but most of the residents in Superior didn't know it. Hell, they didn't even know it was built and launched right in their hometown port, along with nearly forty others, or that it was the last one of its kind in the entire world.

There were a few people putting on the mini golf course, and a couple of moms sitting on the benches near the play area, watching their toddlers. Nobody noticed Rita walking around the bow of the land-berthed ship. Hardly anybody paid enough attention to know there was a wide strip of lush, green lawn between the ship and water's edge, shored up against the hull by a retaining wall. It had a perfect sunset view of the bay.

Rita sank down onto the grass. She set her phone on the ground beside her and stretched her legs out in front of her. She kicked off her flat, ballet-style shoes. She was still wearing the same clothes she'd worn to Sean Nolan's funeral, but she had added a light gray cardigan buttoned up to the top.

She sat there in the glow of the setting sun, cooled by the breeze blowing across the frigid water of the big lake. For the first time that day, she felt she wasn't dressed too warmly for the weather. The sound of the waves soothed her. She drew her knees up, wrapping her arms around them and resting her head on the hard pillow they made.

She waited for Rick's call. She liked Rick—a lot, but she didn't know if they could hold it together much longer. Their relationship was hard enough as it was. Now this case was complicating things even more, and he didn't even know about Pops withholding evidence in the Baker case. What would he do when he found *that* out?

Rita sat bolt upright. "I can't tell him," she said out loud. She knew if he decided to protect Pops because of their relationship he'd be putting his own job on the line. And if he didn't, Pops could be facing criminal charges for knowingly concealing evidence. He'd be an accessory after the fact, and there's no statute of limitations in a homicide.

Her phone rang. She picked it up without looking at the number. "Hey," she said.

"Where are you?" Rick asked her right off.

"I'm sitting out on Barker's Island, watching the sun set."

"I'll be there in fifteen minutes."

He knew where to find her. When you can't go on public dates, you spend a lot of time sitting out under the stars in places most people don't think of.

By the time he arrived, the city lights were twinkling on the Duluth hillside, casting their reflections in rippled brush-strokes of light on the water. Rick sat down beside her on the cool grass. "I take back everything I ever said about your amateur sleuthing. Do you realize what you've done?"

"Yeah, I got lucky because a teenage girl made the mistake of confiding in me."

"Are you kidding me? We, *you*, just got the biggest break in the Baker case ever. Fifty years—fifty years and you stumble over it."

"I'm really sorry you had to cancel your plans to visit Jane," Rita said.

"Is that what's eating you? Don't worry about it, I mean, the girls were disappointed, but I told them we'd go next weekend. They understand my job. Besides, they both had other plans ten minutes after I cancelled the trip."

"So what did Kristy tell you?"

"All the same stuff she told you, I imagine. But his friends filled in the missing details. Sean found a folding knife buried in the dirt floor under a piece of rotted framing in the tool shed. He was in a hurry, pushing the mower back into the shed when it got hung up on the threshold. He kept shoving it and the board cracked in two. He was trying to fit it back together so nobody would notice when he found the knife. I checked the tool shed. The threshold was broken and hobbled back together. I sent an evidence team to go over it with a fine-toothed comb."

"Are you supposed to be telling me this?"

"I owe you," he said. "And I know you won't print a word of until I give the go-ahead."

"That's a switch."

"Rita, I wouldn't have this information if it wasn't for you. Not one of those little punks gave me anything on the knife when I questioned them the night Sean went missing, the *same kids* I questioned again after we found his body."

"They were too scared by that time," Rita said. "Afraid of what would happen to them for not telling somebody about the knife sooner. So did you find it? Was it at his house?"

"Unfortunately, not. And his parents said they never saw him with it."

"That's just what Pops figured." She turned away from the view of the twinkling hillside to look at Rick, her arms still wrapped around her knees. "I told him what happened. I wanted to know what he'd made of it. He said if it really was the knife, it would tie the two homicides together. He thinks whoever killed Sean Nolan wanted that knife in a bad way."

"I think that's the most probable scenario."

"Can we quit pretending, Rick? You know my father told me that Thomas Baker's ear was severed. It was the fact they held back and the reason why they wanted to find that knife. Whoever killed Nolan knew what it had been used for, so I'm going to ask once more. Did somebody cut Sean Nolan's ear off too? Is that what really ties these two homicides together?"

"No."

Rita was so ready for an argument that his quick answer threw her off her game. "Wait, what?" she asked.

"Sean Nolan's ears were both present and accounted for."

"So why the over-reaction at the Spirit Room last night?"

"Because the Baker case is still unsolved. Because you and I together are a lawsuit and two tanked careers waiting to happen. If *anything* like that ever gets out we both know where it ends. And because knowing something that the killer knows is dangerous—as evidenced by Sean Nolan's recent death."

"Why do you think the killer would hide the knife there?"

"I don't think he hid it. I think there was probably a scuffle. The knife could easily have gotten kicked under the framing, or dragged under there if somebody was pulling a dead body out over the threshold."

"I think it was Father Jim." Rita said. "Pops does, too."

"Why Father Jim? I mean, other than the fact that he had opportunity. What would his motive be?"

"An accident, maybe."

"Then why cut the kid's ear off?" Rick asked.

"Couldn't tell you that." Rita hoped her response sounded flippant, more like an *I have no idea* comment than *I know but won't tell you*."

"What does your Pops think?"

Rita thought for a moment, she didn't want to give away too much. "Drugs."

"Not my first thought." Rick said.

"Look, Rick, you've made me sit through enough flag waving, glory, guts and gore war movies to know that it was Vietnam vets who were cutting ears off. Somebody had to have made the same conclusion back then."

"It didn't exactly narrow the suspect list at the time. But Father Jim is too young, couldn't have been in 'Nam yet when Baker was killed."

"What if he was hanging around with a bunch of war protesters, disillusioned veterans? Really, when you think about it, who *didn't* know about the atrocities in Vietnam at the time?"

"Actually, most people. It wasn't really common knowledge then. None of that came out until later in the war. What else did your grandfather tell you about the Baker case?" Rick asked.

Rita's gut fluttered. Had she said too much? Rick was good at his job. He knew how to read between the lines. "Nothing, just about the ear."

"See, that's kind of odd to me, because there's more he could have told you, other things I've read in the case file that weren't public knowledge."

Rita dropped her knees down to sit cross-legged, turning her body to fully face Rick. It was getting dark and she couldn't really make out his features anymore. "Baker *was* molested, wasn't he?"

"No, at least not according to the M.E's report. But there were more wounds than the mortal blow and the missing ear."

"Stab wounds?" Rita tried to make sense of what she was hearing."

"Multiple."

"And Pops knew this? He knew it was murder all along?"

"Not necessarily. They could have been inflicted post mortem."

"Jesus, why?"

"Well, a few reasons. Psychosis, for starters, somebody not quite right upstairs."

Rita cringed.

"But it's unlikely in this case," he said.

"Why?" Rita asked.

"If it was somebody off his nut, there would've been more bodies racked up. It's the kind of thing a serial killer does."

"There's Sean."

"Too many years between."

"Unless the killer was gone, living somewhere else all these years, like Father Jim."

"Like Father Jim, true. But I spent all afternoon checking him out. As far as I can determine, there were no similar, unsolved homicides in any of the places he's lived—but there are a few gaps, times when his whereabouts wasn't known."

"But you checked. So you do suspect him?"

"I've got a few suspects," Rick said. "Let me ask you something. Why did your grandfather tell you about the ear?"

He'd asked her once already, but he made this time sound like the first. *Another interrogation tactic.*

"I wore him down," Rita said. That was the truth.

"Why the ear, and not the rest?"

"I just . . ." Rita paused, her mind racing to figure out where Rick was going. If she didn't stay at least one step ahead, he'd trip her up. "I really don't know. You'd have to ask him that."

"Or, I could tell you another reason somebody would inflict wounds after death?"

"Sure, I guess so."

"To confuse the investigation, to make it look like somebody other than themselves did it. The ear is about as obvious as it can be. It points a finger right to somebody who served in 'Nam. But like I said, that covers about every fourth man between the ages of 18 and 25 at the time."

"Yes, you did say that already."

"The other wounds, though, they don't make sense in that context. They're random, they're a mistake, sloppy. The kind of thing that wins the D.A. convictions."

"I don't follow you."

"There's something else about the puncture wounds," Rick said.

"What?" Rita asked.

"Somebody making them might injure themselves. It's a long shot that they'd do much more than go home and put a few bandages on, but a cop's got to cover all the bases so I checked out the emergency room records for a forty-eight hour period after Thomas Baker disappeared."

Rita stared at Rick's barely distinguishable outline against the dark ship, wishing she could make out more of the nuances in his facial expression. "And you found something?"

"Francis Sullivan, your father, was admitted for treatment of a drug overdose at 10:05 the morning Thomas Baker went missing."

"Yeah, my father had a drug problem. I've never hidden that."

"He also had numerous cuts and contusions, several on his hands."

"And I'm sure you know, from the same records, his injuries were from a motorcycle accident."

"Yes, I read that. How did you know?"

"My grandfather told me."

"When?"

Rita started to answer, then stopped abruptly. "What difference does that make?"

"Not a bit, if it's something you've known for a long time. If you just found out about it recently, I guess I'd wonder why it came up now, what's the significance?"

"I've known. For a long time, okay? My aunt told me how horrible it was, traumatic for her to see her brother all banged up and bloodied with road rash, raving like a maniac because of the drugs and then collapsing in an unconscious heap on the floor." Rita was totally making it up as she went along, but she thought it sounded good.

"I thought you said your grandfather told you."

He'd tripped her up already. She'd have to be more careful. "He did, a long time ago. He didn't like talking about it. I had to get most of the details from my aunt."

"And when your aunt told you, did she remember that it was the same day Thomas Baker disappeared and then showed up later in a ditch? Did she ever wonder if the motorcycle accident involved a kid on a skateboard?"

"No."

"Odd, because you didn't seem surprised when I told you it was the same day."

Got her again. "I'm more surprised that you're trying to lead me by the nose to this ridiculous conclusion you've obviously made. Tell me, then, how you explain Sean Nolan, because my father is dead. You remember that, right? That he died when I was four?" She couldn't believe she'd just played the sympathy card.

"Yeah. I remember that," Rick said. "He put his car into the river, off the same bridge where we found Sean Nolan's body six days ago. I pulled the records on that too. The autopsy on your father showed a blood alcohol just short of rendering him unconscious, not to mention the barbiturates. His death lists blunt force brain injury as result of the accident. There were no apparent signs of braking, no skid marks on the road. I suppose he might have passed out behind the wheel."

"But?" Rita asked, knowing the answer.

"But it might have been suicide. The M.E. couldn't rule it out."

"Your point?"

"Your grandfather was on the desk the night the call came in reporting Baker's body. He sent two uniforms out, no detectives."

"Yeah, well, that's something that's bothered him ever since. It was annual Guard training, half the force was gone for two weeks of camp. That's why he was manning the desk. It was a bad call. He should have put a rookie on the desk and gone out himself."

"Your father's movement that night is suspect. Your grandfather, a seasoned detective, stays on the desk and sends rookies out into the field. Further, he neglects to mention this fact in his sketchy report, a man whose case notes were normally so detailed they read like court transcripts. Less than a year later, he resigns from the department. Ten years later, your brother puts his car in the drink. I gotta say, looking at it all together like that, it makes me wonder."

"Talk about a fishing expedition," Rita said.

"Oh, wait. There's one more thing," Rick said. "A piece of evidence central to this case shows up fifty years later, on the property of the church your father and grandfather both attended. I have to ask, Rita, what is it you're not telling me?"

XV

Could this day have any more highs and lows? Rick was pumping her for information about a crime her father may have committed and her grandfather covered up. She couldn't take anymore.

"Fuck you, Rick. Fuck you ten ways to hell." Rita rose to her feet and started walking away.

Rick sprang up and grabbed her elbow before she could make her escape. "Wait. Hear me out."

She couldn't listen to another word. He was too close to the truth and she was close to breaking down. She wanted to just lay it all at his feet and let the astute Detective Drake, SPD's own closer, hone in on the one detail everybody else had missed, the one fact that ruled out her father. But what if that fact didn't exist?

"I don't want to hear another word," she yelled at him. "You're insane! Let go of me."

Rick didn't release her. "Whoever killed Sean Nolan wanted that knife, probably tried to get it away from him and there was a struggle," Rick said.

Rita stopped pulling against his grip, but wouldn't give him the satisfaction of turning around to look at him. This was no polite conversation. It was an inquiry. "God, you sound just like him."

"Like who?"

"My grandfather. That's exactly the same thing Pops said about Thomas Baker. What's so fucking special about that knife that two kids got killed over it?"

Rick let go of her arm. "Not both, just one. Nobody knows why Thomas Baker was killed, but it seems odd your grandfather would project a story onto that crime, one that seems the more possible scenario for the Nolan case."

"No." Rita actually stamped her foot. She had to do something physical and it was better than punching Rick in the face. "No, that's not what happened. My Pops did not kill Sean Nolan. I'm telling you, it didn't happen. He's eighty-six years old. How would he snap that kid's neck? How would he get him to the river and throw him off a bridge?"

The whole time she was wondering if that was exactly what happened, if Pops was so desperate to protect his own son, even in death, that he'd tried to get the knife away from Sean Nolan and something went horribly wrong.

"Two nights ago you were trying to convince me a man his age could do just that, but that's not what I'm saying."

She didn't want to listen; she didn't want to hear him connect the dots that all led to her father and grandfather being complicit in the murder of the two boys, but she couldn't move. A stronger force than Rick's grip was holding her back. She wanted to know the truth.

"Rita, I'm going to suggest something and I want you to stay as calm as you can. Have you considered that your grandfather might have been involved in Thomas Baker's death?"

"Involved, how?" Rita asked, bracing herself for the blowback.

"Father Jim told me about his temper. I think it's possible he stopped the Baker kid for some infraction, things got out of hand. Maybe he pushed him, and the kid hit his head."

Rita couldn't believe what she was hearing. *He wasn't even close.* She wanted to gloat, but she took a deep breath, forcing everything down into her belly.

She turned slowly, "Wow. And all this time I thought you were a good cop, a smart cop. You're just grasping at straws. First you tell me it's possible my father killed Thomas Baker, and now you're changing your tune? Now you think my *grandfather* brutalized a fourteen-year-old boy?"

"Based on what you told me here, tonight, yes. It's one possible scenario. It could have happened right there on the refinery road. Maybe he stopped the kid to warn him about riding in traffic. Or maybe he caught Baker bumper cruising. The kid gives him lip—you said he was a smart aleck. Pops tries to take him into custody, take him down to the station to put a little scare in him, make his parents come pick him up."

"And bashes him over the head and for good measure? Turns him into a human pincushion? And then cuts his ear off? Explain that one."

"Drugs."

Rita laughed out loud. "You've completely lost it. I don't even know who you are. My grandfather, out of his mind on drugs?"

"No, to make it look like a drug-crazed killer. What better way to ensure that the last person anybody would connect to such a heinous and poorly executed crime would be a cop?"

"Sure, Sherlock. That's how it happened. And then my Pops went home, went about his day, and reported for night duty as desk sergeant so he could take the call reporting Baker's body."

"Rita. I'm going to have to question your grandfather."

She shook her head back and forth in slow motion. "Unbelievable." For the first time since she'd try to flee she was looking him right in the eyes. "You're going to put my eighty-six year old grandfather in jail? You jerk."

"Jail? Who said anything about jail? I simply want to talk to him, at his place, with you there."

"Do me a favor. Stop thinking I have any idea of ever helping you with this. My grandfather didn't kill Thomas Baker *or* Sean Nolan. End of conversation."

"How do you know that Rita? What do you know that makes you so sure?"

What the hell. Go for broke. "Because up until a few hours ago, my grandfather was convinced it *was* my *father*."

Rick didn't react at all. She expected surprise, or at least a modicum of interest. His utterly calm demeanor unnerved her, like waiting for the proverbial shoe to drop.

"Well?" She asked. "No *ah-ha*?"

He remained silent, using her own tactics against her. That's how she got the good information for a story.

Oh fuck, how could I be so stupid? she thought. "Did you just play me?" She asked.

Still no response from him. He was good at this.

"You did. I can't believe I fell for *that!* I'm outta here." She took a few steps, then turned back, a little surprised that he wasn't trying to stop her this time. "You think my father killed Thomas Baker, don't you?"

"Rita—"

Now he wanted to talk. "Save it. I guess all good cops think alike. It took you all of two seconds after seeing those emergency room records to jump to the same conclusion my Pops did. You never suspected my grandfather at all and I fell for it like a john falls for an underage tart with a fake I.D."

"Rita, I'm sorry. I knew I'd never be able to crack your grandfather. He knows all the tricks."

"Stupid, stupid, stupid," Rita admonished herself.

"I have to know if there's anything else you've been keeping from me?"

"No."

"Stop being so stubborn. I want to help you."

"No, I haven't been keeping anything else." Rita said.

"What changed your grandfather's mind about your father's guilt?"

"What?"

"You said until a few hours ago. What happened a few hours ago?"

"The knife."

If she told him it was the alleged confession that tipped Pops off to her father's innocence, he'd shoot the defense full of holes. It wouldn't be hard to do, she knew herself that memories lost in drunken blackouts often found their way back. Besides, if she told him, he'd be holding all the cards and right now, she didn't relish that idea. So she lied to him, with no compunction. *The apple doesn't fall far after all,* she thought.

"Whoever killed Sean doesn't want that knife found because it might expose Baker's killer. It wouldn't be my father, because he's dead. And Pops wouldn't do it to protect his son because, again, he's dead; what's to protect?" She wasn't a praying woman, but at that moment, she prayed to God, Goddess, the universe—it didn't matter; she prayed that what she was saying was true.

Rick was shaking his head. "There *had* to be more. Dave Sullivan wouldn't suspect his own kid just because he was a drug addict, or because of some motorcycle accident. He had to have more, Rita. What was it? And what about it has changed?"

"If there was anything else, he kept his suspicions to himself." Rita was determined not to give Rick one more bit of information.

"What about your Uncle Stan?" Rick asked

"Stan? What does he have to do with any of this?"

"He and your grandfather are pretty close, aren't they?"

"Yes."

"Close enough that your Uncle Stan might do anything for him?"

"Jesus, what is this, some kind of a witch-hunt on my entire family? Like there's not another single person in this whole town to pin this on? Next you'll be accusing me."

"Don't be ridiculous, Rita."

"Ridiculous? Any more ridiculous than my grandfather mutilating a dead boy's body to throw suspicion off himself? More ridiculous than my father, just a kid himself, committing a brutal murder?"

She didn't let Rick answer her. She was rolling like an engine with a full head of steam.

"Wait. I know. Maybe we're all in on it together, a whole family of sociopaths. Did you think about that, huh? Maybe that's why I started sleeping with you in the first place, so you'd never be able to rat us out without bringing an ugly scandal down on your own head."

"Rita, I know you're upset—"

"You *think*? What was your first clue, detective?"

"Please, Rita, for once can you just listen and not question," he said.

"No. I really don't want to listen to anything else you have to say." This time she meant it. He had nothing that was going to help her.

"Rita, I have to talk to your grandfather. I want you to be there."

"Fat chance."

"If we don't find that knife again, and find it soon, this case is going as cold as the Baker case. Hell, even if we do find the knife, it's been so many years there might not be anything left to help us—if there ever was anything."

"I'm sorry. This has all gotten a little too crazy for me. Maybe these deaths don't have a single thing to do with one another. I'm the brilliant one who came up with that theory—and what the hell do I know? Oh, and let's not forget that two days before Sean Nolan was killed, I laid out the whole Baker case in print for everybody to read."

"I told you, Rita, that wouldn't be enough to trigger Baker's killer into striking again."

"No, just enough for somebody to use it, to cover a completely random crime. That's what you told me the first day, standing on the bridge."

"That was before you told me your grandfather suspected his own son. I'm going to have to question him, Rita. I think it's important for you to be there when I do. For us."

Rita's chest tightened; her stomach quivered. "Yeah, well as my dear Grandma Abby used to say, shit in one hand and wish in the other, then see which one gets filled first." She left him standing on the dark side of the ship, practically running around the bow into the light of the parking lot.

She was furious, playing out a dozen arguments and denials in her head, telling Rick off with a rapier wit she hadn't been able to muster when they were face to face. And what was with that declaration, *important for us*? Us, like there was a future for that pronoun in their relationship.

She arrived at her apartment surprised to be there, barely remembering the drive home from Barker's Island. She let herself in and sat on the sofa in the semi-darkness, staring out the window, watching nothing. The old halogen street light on the corner cast a glow like moonlight into room, bringing the outside in. Not light, not dark. Not in, not out. She felt like she was caught in the Twilight Zone. Everybody was telling her a different story. They couldn't all be true, so who was lying?

She sank back against the soft pillows on her sofa, her head pounding from the confusion of jumbled thoughts. What was it Pops had said about the janitor at the church? He was a good man with a family, kids to feed? *There's an element of truth in every lie.*

Rick's outrageous hypothesis caught her off guard, got her to spill the truth, or part of it anyway. *Probably lack of sleep,* she thought. She couldn't remember the last time she'd slept soundly, or more than a few hours at a time.

Rick had planted a seed and now it was germinating. What if his crazy scenario had an element of truth in it? Was *Pops* responsible for the Baker boy's death? What if he'd made up the whole story he told her? How did Rita even know that Pops actually found Baker's ear in his brief case? Or that he told Uncle Stan all of this years ago? They were thick as thieves. Stan might not kill for him, but he'd probably lie.

She sat up. Her thoughts were suddenly starting to line up and follow one another in some kind of order. Pops would never tell a lie that would implicate his son to cover for himself.

The stab wounds put a new spin on things. What if it was self-defense? What if Thomas Baker tried to attack Rita's father with the knife. And in the struggle, he fell and hit his head, and . . .

"GOD!" She yelled into the darkness. "That's as bat-shit crazy as everything Rick said." She grabbed a pillow from the sofa and threw it against the opposite wall. Two dead bodies, an ear, a missing knife found, and now missing again. How did it all fit together?

She kicked at the leg of the coffee table and stomped across the floor to the back door, feeling the wall for the bank of light switches. She flipped on the overhead lights. She wanted to talk to Pops. She wanted to demand answers—better answers than she had been given up to now.

She felt the sobs rising from her chest, into her throat. She held her breath, strangling them of the air they needed to cry out, until her throat ached. She just wanted Pops to fix this, to make it all go away.

She went to the kitchen, took the bottle of Bombay out of her freezer and poured herself a glassful. Back on the sofa, she picked up her phone; there was a text message. She must have missed it earlier.

She tapped the screen to bring it up, immediately bringing Pops's I.D. into the window. The message was short and to the point.

`Let sleeping dogs lie or you might get bitten.`

XVI

She stared at the text message. Rita had told Pops he didn't have to learn all the functions on his cell phone when she gave it to him, but he insisted. What was the point of having something you didn't use?

Still, a text from Pops was unusual. True, he'd been in a mood when she left him. It wasn't often that he let her get by with reversing their roles that way, ordering him to stay put. The text was probably a way to scold her, to reassert his authority without having to listen to any sass.

She checked the timestamp on the message. He'd sent it almost as soon as she left his place. Did Pops go to the rectory to confront Father Jim after all? Did Jim tell Pops something that made him want to keep the lid on this more than ever?

Let sleeping dogs lie, or you might get bitten. The more she read it, the more it sounded to her like a threat.

Obviously exhaustion was robbing her brain of the oxygen it needed to think straight. To prove it, she heard her Grandma Abby's voice and wasn't sure if it was all in her head or if Grandma's spirit was whispering in her ear. *Trust your Pops, Rita. He'll never steer you wrong.*

Rita looked back at the number, like it might have somehow changed. Nope, it was Pops's all right.

She tried to put herself in his place, tried to empathize with Pops's instinct to protect his son at almost any cost. It wasn't easy for her. Rita never made a conscious choice to forgo motherhood; it just didn't happen in the years she was with Mark and she'd never thought about it as a problem to be remedied. Now she realized her utter lack of maternal instincts was just another black stain on her soul–at least according to her ex-husband.

She checked the time on the phone. It was almost eleven PM. She weighed the odds of Pops being asleep like he'd said he'd be. Her finger hovered above his speed dial number.

This could wait until morning. Her finger touched the number key lightly for a moment and then she pressed it down and found herself hearing the ring. It went straight to Pops's voice mail. Either his phone was charging, or he'd shut it off. She tried a second time, waiting for the connection. Same thing.

The urge to just fall into bed and let sleep overtake her was a powerful temptation, but it wasn't going to happen. She could tell herself that Pops was safe and sound in his bed where he should be, but she wasn't going to convince herself. *May as well go back out now and get it over with.*

The walk would do her good. She grabbed her keys and phone from the coffee table. She was almost at the back door when she heard what sounded like footsteps coming from the front porch. She walked quietly back across the room to the hallway that led to the front door. From there, she could hear the soft creak of the porch's old floorboards.

Who would be on her front porch at this time of night? Certainly nobody who knew her—everybody she knew used her back door. Somebody looking for the tenants upstairs, maybe?

Rita listened for the sound again, standing still as the second hand on a broken watch. The door handle turned, slowly at first, then faster, back and forth. The door was always locked—all the tenants had a key. She heard the solid oak thumping against the frame. It had been pushed and pulled with considerable force.

Her heart raced. She lunged for the wall switch and turned off the lights. Then she glanced over to the window that was always open during the summer. The streetlight on the corner lit up the full length of that side of the house. Nobody would have the guts to go prowling around that window. *Would they?*

She dropped down to her knees, her stomach twisting in fear and her heart pounding inside her chest. The doorknob stopped turning. The footsteps moved along the length of the porch, across the front of her apartment. She was in a direct line with her bedroom doorway, and the room's narrow window overlooked the porch. The window blind was pulled halfway down. She watched, frozen in terror while a pair of silhouetted legs walked into the frame.

She heard the glass pane rattle with the effort of trying to lift the sash. She flattened herself to the floor, wishing to disappear, hoping if she were quiet enough and invisible enough, whoever it was would just go away. Her heart was beating so furiously she could feel it pounding against the floor.

She was aware of the phone in her hand, but fear was telling her not to utter a sound, not even a call for help. She *wanted* to call Rick, but who knew where he was now, or if he would even answer after she'd told him to fuck off. The police station was only three blocks away—they could have a patrol car here in less than a minute.

That fact comforted her, and with a small measure of relief came rational thinking. *The police station is only three blocks away. A random burger isn't going to target a house just up the street from a whole force of cops.*

Whoever was on her porch *did* know her, or at least knew where she lived.

She took a deep breath, tightened her abdomen in and yelled as loud as she could. "Who's out there?"

The window stopped rattling and she saw the legs step back. She'd startled whoever it was, but they weren't running.

"I'm dialing 9-1-1 right now!" she yelled.

The legs turned and she heard quick steps retreating from the porch. She stood and ran into her bedroom, looking out the window, but whoever had been on her porch had already cleared the front yard and the fence surrounding it.

Rita pulled the shade down and sat on the edge of her bed, forcing her breathing back to normal. She closed her eyes, trying to bind the image of the legs to her memory, but there wasn't much to work with. A pair of pants from just below the waist to just above the knees. They could have been loose jeans, or trousers. There was no point in calling the police now. Dark colored pants wasn't much of a description to go on.

Things were suddenly very real. This game of amateur detective she'd been playing was no game at all. She had flushed out a killer. Now what?

She remembered the open window in the living room and her pulse quickened again. Tiptoeing out of her bedroom, she skirted the living room with her back to the wall, sidling up to the bank of three windows. She turned quickly, covering the distance to the center window, pulled it down and locked it. Then she lowered each shade down to the sill, wondering if the stalker was still out there, watching her tremble with fear, chuckling with satisfaction. He'd know by now that there were no cops on the way.

Rita checked the locks on her back door, turned on the light over the stove and pulled the shade down over the kitchen window before returning to the living room. She curled into the corner of the sofa with a blanket pulled around her, clutching it up to her chin, trying to quell the shivers that were shaking her from head to toe.

She picked up her phone and dialed Pops's number again hoping he'd answer, wanting to feel the comfort of his voice. Not only the reassurance that he was home and safe, but that all was right in her world as long as Pops was there. For the third time, it went straight to his voice mail.

She sat immobile, listening for the smallest noise and gathering her courage to get off the sofa. Finally, she stood up slowly, and then made her way to the back door. She turned the lock, opening the door just enough to peer out into the yard. Then she stepped onto the porch, quickly locked the door behind her and raced to her car.

The drive to Pops's place took only minutes, but when she arrived, his car was not in its usual parking space. "Damn, Pops. Where the hell are you?"

She rounded the block coming back out onto 12th Street towards Grand Avenue away from her apartment and headed out to the waterfront. She'd look for Pops's car at Immaculate Heart. *What if it's there,* she thought? *It's late, he wouldn't still be there if it was a friendly visit.* "Do I call the cops?" she asked herself out loud.

There was no sign of Pops's Camry on the street or in the lot. The rectory was dark inside. There was only one other place she could think to look—Uncle Stan's.

She drove past the front of the small apartment building, around to the side. Stan never parked his beloved Elky on the street. It was always tucked safe and sound in his assigned garage stall. But if Pops *was* there, she'd see the Camry nosed up to the single width door.

Pops's car was there all right, but to her surprise, Stan's Camino was out on the street. Maybe they'd gone out together earlier. But even if they took Elky, Pops would have parked out on the street so Stan had free access out of the garage and then in again when they returned.

Rita was beginning to get the picture. Pops wasn't about to sit home because she told him to. He'd probably called Stan to grouse about it, and between the two of them, they settled on showing her a thing or two by meeting up at one of their old watering holes, Pudge's, no doubt.

After lifting elbows for a while, Pops figured he'd had one too many to drive home all the way across town. He took the lesser risk of driving a few blocks to Stan's place. He must have beat Stan there and parked right up next to the garage door out of habit. *Damn fool drunks.*

Rita decided to just go home. She'd deal with Pops in the morning. But the windows in Stan's apartment were all lit up. If she knew those two clowns, the bottle of slivo came out as soon as they got in the door. They were probably still at it, or they'd passed out with the lights on. Either way she'd better check on them. She parked her bug behind Elky and cut the engine.

XVII

Stan's apartment was on the third floor, across from the elevator and down the hall. From the best she could remember, it was where the 5th and 6th grade classrooms had been before the building got converted to apartments. She could hear Pops's and Stan's loud voices as she got nearer to the door. *They must really have a snoot full.*

She rapped on the door and turned the knob to open it at the same time, the standard operating procedure when calling on old men with deaf ears. "Uncle Stan, Pops? It's just me, Rita," she called out.

"Go away, Rita. Don't come in."

What the hell? It was Stan's voice. She hesitated a brief moment out of respect. Maybe they weren't decent.

"Pops, what's going on? Are you drunk?"

"No, Rita. I'm perfectly sober. Your Uncle Stan and I are just talking, that's all. You should go home."

"I'm coming in, Pops."

"No. Rita. Just close the door and go home." Pops's voice was more urgent this time.

Rita pushed the door open. "What the hell is going on in here?"

Pops was standing, facing her. Stan was sitting at the table, partially hidden behind Pops. Something wasn't right.

"Rita. Listen to me. Your Uncle Stan, he . . . well, he was out drinking. Had a little too much."

"Stan?" Rita's tone begged for his validation of Pops's story. "Is that right?"

"Yeah, yeah. I got a little carried away."

"He called me to come get him. I drove him home in my car, then I walked back over and picked up his Camino so the whole neighborhood wouldn't see it sitting there tomorrow. We're good here. You should just go home and get some rest."

"Pops, did you go over to the rectory tonight? Did you talk to Father Jim?"

"She's too smart for you, Dave. You raised her too smart, and she's always a step ahead."

Pops laughed. It sounded forced. "Yeah, whatever you say, Stan." He rolled his eyes and mimed drinking too much, then waved Rita away with both hands.

"Too smart for what?" Rita asked.

"I'll tell you all about it in the morning Rita. I'm going to sit with Stan until he's feeling a little better. Maybe I'll even stay here tonight; it's getting pretty late."

"I'll sit with you for a while, then, too." Rita took a few steps forward.

Pops blocked her.

"Pops—what's going on?"

"Rita, I wish you'd listen to me, just this once. Go home. We're fine here."

"No, you're not. Something's not right." She sidestepped her grandfather. Stan was sitting with both elbows resting on the table, his hands together just in front of his chest. He was hunched forward, his head down. He almost looked like he was praying. "Oh for God's sake, were you in a fight, Uncle Stan? Let me see your face."

He lifted his head, turning slowly, pivoting from his waist. His left shoulder and arm came around and his right hand went down to the table. There wasn't a mark on his face.

Rita stared in confusion. Then, her vision slowly widened. She followed the line of his right arm to the table, where his hand rested on a revolver.

"Jesus Christ. What the hell, Uncle Stan?"

"I told you to go home, Rita." Pops said.

"Stan? What the hell are you doing with that gun?"

"Go home Rita," Stan said. "This doesn't concern you."

"I'm not going home. Quit telling me to go home."

"By all means, then," Stan said. "Sit down and join the party." The facial tic pulled at his cheek.

"Will one of you please tell me what in the name of God is going on here?"

"Go ahead, Dave. Tell her how you're planning to throw me under the bus."

"Why don't you give me that gun now, Stan? You don't want to hurt anybody—especially not Rita."

"Rita? Why would I hurt Rita?"

"You wouldn't. Of course you wouldn't. But just to be safe."

Rita's head was spinning. Her purse was still slung over her shoulder. She took a few slow steps over to the table and sank into an empty chair, letting the bag fall to her lap. She wondered if she could reach inside, find her phone and manage to punch the right number on the keypad to speed dial Rick. That was about a chance in a million, and if she somehow succeeded they'd all be able to hear Rick's voice answering.

Pops was still standing, trying to maintain some control over the situation—whatever the situation was. Sweat beaded on his mostly bald head like a string of pearls where his hairline used to be.

"Your Pops was here waiting for me when I came in."

"From the bar? So you drove yourself home?" Rita was still confused.

"There was no bar, Rita," Pops said. "Well, at least I wasn't at the bar. You, Stan?"

"No."

"Okay. Enough," Rita said. "I'll ask the questions."

"There you go, Dave. She'll ask the questions. The smart reporter will figure it all out. Just give her time."

"Rita. Leave this to me," Pops said.

She was about to object when Pops locked his eyes on hers. She bit back her retort.

"I came here to ask your Uncle Stan a few questions. I think I upset him a little, that's all."

That was an understatement if she'd ever heard one. "I was just trying to calm him down when you arrived," she said.

"Your grandfather has been busy tonight, Rita."

"So it seems," she said.

"He called me after you left, asked me to come to his place. He wanted my help convincing you to drop all this nonsense of getting to the bottom of the Baker case. We'd thought after we told you your father might be involved, you'd back off. But you didn't. Even the possibility that your Pops might be charged and could go to jail didn't scare you off."

"I haven't told a soul about that. I would never hurt Pops."

"You hear that, Dave? Just like you, protecting her own."

"Leave her out of it, Stan."

Stan kept talking. "So tonight I tried to convince your Pops that the only thing left to do was to scare you good, really put the fear of God in you. But he balked at that and told me to get out."

"Scare me? How?"

Stan laughed. "With a little prowling around in the dark."

"That was you on my porch tonight?"

Pops took his eyes off of Stan long enough look at Rita. "What? When?"

"Somebody was at my house tonight, trying to get in the front door, then the bedroom window—or at least trying to make me think that."

"What time tonight?" Pops asked her.

"I don't know, after you texted me. Around eleven or so. I called but you didn't answer, so I decided to make sure you were okay. Before I could leave, somebody was prowling around on my front porch, rattling my door and window."

"I didn't send you a text," Pops said.

"It was your number. Don't poke a sleeping dog?" She paused. "You might get bitten?"

"You wouldn't listen to me, Dave," Stan said. "I told you we had to find a way to scare her off. And it worked. You know that open window you're always warning her about? You don't have to worry anymore. It's closed now, and locked too."

"You sent Rita a threatening text, from my phone? When?"

"When I was at your place. You went into the kitchen. I picked it up off the table and sent the message. Then I shut it off so she couldn't call you back."

"For Christ's sake, Stan. It didn't occur to you that eventually she'd ask me about the message?"

Pops was cursing. For the first time since she'd sat down, Rita felt more scared than confused. She looked to see what Stan was wearing: trousers that fit much looser than his standard, trim cut jeans. "Did you have that gun with you when you were standing out on my porch, Uncle Stan?"

"No. I didn't have the gun with me. I might be a little misguided, but I'm not stupid enough to do something like that," he said. "Is that really what you think of me?" His voice rose a notch.

"Take it easy now, Stan. She wasn't accusing you of anything," Pops said.

"Rita, I'd never hurt you. I just thought . . . You wouldn't let it alone. Even after we told you about Frankie. Even after you knew that blowing the lid off of this whole thing might send your grandfather to jail."

"Is that what this is about? You're trying to protect Pops from me, with that gun? Was that the next step in your plan to scare me off?"

"Rita, no." Pops said. "That's not what's happening. Just leave this to me. You have to trust me."

"You should listen to him, Rita. He's just trying to take care of you. That's what he does, you know. He takes care of everybody."

"That's right Stan. And I want to take care of you, too. I will, if you just give me that gun," Pops said. "I promise."

"Then what, Dave? What do we all do tomorrow? Pretend none of this happened? Go on pretending none of it *ever* happened?"

"None of *what*?" Rita demanded.

Both men ignored her.

"We'll figure that out tomorrow, Stan," Pops said. "Right now, you just have to give me that gun."

"You told me everything would be okay once before, but it wasn't. It was never okay."

Uncle Stan's mouth was twitching after almost every word, his eyes shimmering with manic excitement.

"Everybody always looked up to you, always thought you were so good. But they didn't know the truth, did they? They didn't know everything I know."

"Stan, it's ancient history. You have to let it go."

"How many beatings does it take before you're a man, Dave? Three? Ten? Fifty?"

Rita was more confused than ever. Was he talking about Pops and her father, now?

"How many times did I have to get the back of my old man's hand for–" the corner of his mouth pulled into a grotesque, protracted grimace. He struggled to continue speaking. "This!" he finally said, pointing to the facial spasm.

"You were barely three years old when I was drafted to Korea. You didn't have . . . There wasn't any problem then, everything was fine when I left. How was I supposed to know what was going on while I was gone?"

"Are you telling me that you didn't know what your sister married? That you never saw her bruises?"

"Pops. Is that true?" Rita could barely form the words. "You were a cop and you didn't even protect your own sister?" Rita wondered who this man she'd looked up to all her life really was. Then she realized she didn't want to know; she couldn't stand one more disappointment.

"What was I supposed to do, Stan? Take him out back and shoot him? Every time I put in him jail to cool off, she'd come crying to me to let him out, that she loved him and needed him. Tell me. What was I supposed to do?"

"More. You were supposed to do more, Dave. I was just a kid. A little kid," Uncle Stan said.

"I did everything I could. I tried to keep an eye on you. I got you into McCaskill so I could see you every day, see that you were okay."

"You should have gotten me out of that house. You should have kept me from running away to 'Nam."

"For Christ's sake, Stan, you were signed up and gone before any of us knew what you'd done."

"No. You were too busy with own life, going to college, making your perfect family with Abby and your kids. You were too busy being the cop everybody loved, the guy they could count on to do the right thing. Unless the right thing was helping me."

"You had to learn how to stand up for yourself. That was your problem. You expected everything to be easy, to come easy. That was always your problem."

Rita could sense Stan's increasing antagonism. She watched his fingers grasping and releasing the revolver grip. Pops was moving slowly, one step at time, ever closer to him.

"Or was I the mistake nobody ever wanted? Is that it? Born too late after my mother had finally given up on ever having a child? Always in the way, a retarded little SOB?" Stan looked up at Pops. A tear slid down his cheek.

"Stan, what are you saying? I've never felt that way about you." Pops kept moving, leading with his right arm crossed over his chest, holding onto his left arm above the elbow, trying to ease up next to Stan with a nonthreatening posture.

"I just need to know, Dave. Would you have protected me the way you protected Frankie?" Stan asked

"Stan, I'm begging you. Give me that gun before somebody gets hurt."

"You were right about your father, Rita. *Frankie* never had a single thing to do with Thomas Baker's death. Tell her, Dave."

Rita sat stone still.

"Your Pops did pay Father Jim a visit tonight." Stan said. "Tell her, Dave. She wants to know everything, don't you, Rita?"

Pops didn't give her time to answer. "I had something I needed to get off my chest." He absent-mindedly ran his hand back and forth across his chest, just below his collarbone. "Jim Wiese didn't kill Thomas Baker, and he didn't have a clue about the kid's missing ear."

"Go figure," Stan said.

Rita finally found her voice. "How can you be so sure he was telling you the truth? And doesn't that just point the finger back at my father?"

"I just know," Pops said. "It wasn't Father Jim, and it wasn't your father, either."

"But how. How do you know that for sure?"

"I wasn't there to ask questions. I was there to make a confession."

Stan laughed. "A confession. That's perfect. The truth, the whole truth and nothing but the truth straight from the mouth of Dave Sullivan?"

"You made a confession to Father Jim? Like a *bless me father I have sinned* confession?" Rita asked.

"Exactly like that. I sat across from him, looked him right in the eye and I told him that I broke the law, withheld evidence in a major murder case to protect my son. I told him I found a severed ear in my briefcase three days after Thomas Baker's body was found missing that ear."

"And the beauty of it is Father Jim can't tell a soul," Stan said. "He can't break the seal of the confessional. Just like Father Bartoelli could never tell anybody what he knew."

"Bartoelli." Rita barely whispered the name.

"She's almost got it figured out, Dave. Just tell her already."

Rita was watching her grandfather. His shirt was soaked with sweat. His chest rose and fell with short breaths. He kept his eyes on Stan.

Rita suddenly felt nauseous. Everything she ever thought was true about Pops lay crumbled at her feet. Was it possible that Rick had stumbled onto the truth of her grandfather without even knowing it?

"Pops, was it you? Did you make that confession to Father Bartoelli? Did you kill Thomas Baker?"

XVIII

Rita's head was reeling. Pops was becoming more of a monster each minute that ticked by, and Stan had his finger on the trigger of the gun. Had he been trying to force the truth out of Pops when she arrived?

"Tell her, Dave. Tell Rita what finally tipped you off. I'm sure she's curious—I know I am."

Tipped him off? Wait, so not Pops? Rita felt like she was caught in a game of monkey in the middle, but it wasn't a ball Pops and Uncle Stan were tossing back and forth; it was a bomb set to explode the instant she caught it.

"The anonymous call," Pops said. "Reporting the car seen at the church early the morning Baker disappeared."

Rita saw Stan's fingers tighten around the gun grip. "I thought that turned out to be a dead end," she said to Pops.

"Yeah, I thought so too. But after I satisfied myself that Father Jim didn't have a hand in the Baker Case, I left the rectory and went down to the station. Bamboozled some rookie pulling night duty into letting me take a peek at the file on the Baker case by throwing my name around. It was pretty much what I remembered, except for a few details."

"What details?" Rita asked.

"The tip described a tan-colored car with a long, low, front end. Maybe a Cutlass or an Impala. As soon as we released the description a fellow came down to the station driving his Cameo Beige Impala—showed the name of the paint color right on the sales invoice still in the glove box."

Uncle Stan scoffed. "The Cutlass and the Impala didn't look anything alike in '66."

"Maybe not to a gearhead, but a lot of people could make that mistake. He said he drove that car past Immaculate Heart around 6:15 the Sunday morning in question. His kid delivered the Sunday edition of the *Tribune* and he was dropping him off at the start of his route, just a few blocks from the church. It was all in the report."

"So it was a dead end." Rita said. "I don't get it."

"The anonymous caller said it was early when he saw the car there. There were no other cars anywhere around."

"When the driver of the Impala passed by the church at 6:15, there would have been cars all up and down both sides of the street. People going to the 6:30 mass."

"Good catch," Stan said.

"I'm not following you, Pops." Rita's pulse was racing, her face felt hot. She couldn't think about anything but the gun in Uncle Stan's hand.

"It wasn't him, it wasn't a beige Impala. The caller saw somebody else, much earlier in the morning." Pops was getting closer to Stan again, his steps so agonizingly slow it looked as if he were struggling just to move. He had his right arm crossed over his chest, holding onto his left arm, nervously sliding his hand up and down.

"Like I said, a casual observer, might not know the difference between an Impala or a Malibu, or maybe even a Cutlass back then, but do you know what looked like a dead ringer for a Malibu from the front end, Rita?"

"Me? I barely know a Chevy from a Ford," she said.

"An El Camino. Gold, not tan. Just like the one your Uncle Stan bought when he was home on leave, before his second tour in 'Nam."

"Stan?"

"That would have been in the summer of 1966. Right, Stan? You were going back as a Navy Seal—one of the men on the first team. I guess some of those early life lessons toughened you up after all."

"Enough for the Seals to turn me into an efficient machine. Maybe now taking my old man out back and shooting him seems like the better option. Lower body count in the end."

Rita looked at her uncle, unable to grasp all of what she was hearing.

"So what's the verdict?" Stan asked. "Are we going to keep the family secret for another fifty years? Am I worth protecting the way Frankie was when you thought he killed Thomas Baker?"

Rita's head was spinning, literally buzzing. She felt she might faint. "You? You killed Thomas Baker? Why? Why would you do something like that?"

"It was an accident," he said, and then he started laughing.

Rita could only stare at him in horror.

"What's the matter, Rita? You don't see the irony? All these years, your Pops wasn't protecting Frankie, he wasn't even protecting Jim Wiese. It was me all along. The whole time he was protecting *me* and he never even knew it." Stan was practically slapping his knee. "That's a good one, isn't it Dave?"

"How did it happen, Stan?" Pops asked.

"I'm not real clear on that. I remember the knife and he was goofing around with it, pretending like he was one of those little gooks I was killing in 'Nam."

Rita cringed at the slur.

"No, before that. From the beginning," Pops said.

"It was hot. I was driving the Camino around just after dawn with the windows down. I stopped in front of the church, thought I'd maybe go in, talk to God if he existed—get my head straight. But I just sat there on the front steps. I was barely nineteen years old. In another week, I'd be back in that jungle, nowhere to get out of the heat and the stink of burning, rotting flesh. I just wanted to sit there on those steps forever. Then this kid shows up on a skateboard and starts talking to me."

Rita couldn't look at Uncle Stan, but the pained expression on her grandfather's face gave her no solace either.

"He was kind of a smart mouth, but funny. He made me laugh, and I hadn't had much to laugh about for a while. The next thing you know, we're in that tool shed, smoking a little dope. I brought it back with me from 'Nam. I think it might have been laced with acid."

"So you were high." Pops said. "Your judgment was impaired."

Uncle Stan laughed again, "Yeah, we were both wasted. He had that little toy knife—couldn't stab a frog with it if he tried—and he was pretending like he was attacking me."

"So you fought him off?" Pops asked.

"Kind of. You know, just slapping his arm away, deflecting him. I was laughing so hard I nearly pissed myself. That's all I remember. I think I freaked out, flashed back to 'Nam. When I came to my senses he was just laying there. I'd stuck him so many times, but there wasn't much blood."

"He died from the blow to the head," Pops said. "It must have been instantly—heart stopped pumping. Did you hit him with something?"

"I don't know. I couldn't remember. I might have pushed him, knocked him down—maybe I even conked him on the head with a shovel or something. All I knew was he was laying there on his back stuck full of holes."

"How the hell did you get him out of there?" Pops asked. "There had to be people coming and going from mass half the day."

"It was still early, there wasn't anybody around yet. I got the Camino and pulled it up on the street close to the shed. I threw him over my shoulder and put him in the back. I drove around for a while, trying to figure out the best place to dump him. Finally, I just left him in that ditch. I thought for sure it didn't matter, that I was going to get caught. That *somebody* had to have seen me."

"Why did you pull his shirt over his head?"

"I did that when we were still in the shed. His eyes were open, dead you know, but staring at me just the same. Gave me the jeebers."

"And the ear?"

"That fucking ear." He laughed again. "I found it in my pocket–guess I put there when I was still crazy with the drugs, to add to the collection I'd started in 'Nam. But I knew what was going down with you and Frankie. You were riding him to man up, the same way you'd done to me. I wasn't so sure you'd help me out of a bad jam like that, but I bet my life you'd cover for your own kid."

"And you let me think for all these years that it was Frankie. That my son had done this?" Pops looked like he might crumble under the weight of his grief. His face was pinched and his skin was ashen.

"I just wanted to forget it. I put that ear in your briefcase–you never mentioned it to a soul. When a few days passed and it was time for me to head back to 'Nam, I just left."

He looked right at Rita, "Just like Father Jim told you. What was one more innocent body on my hands after all them gooks in the jungle? I even asked Father Bartoelli, when I came home after that second tour. I told him everything I'd done over there with the blessing of the U.S. Government. I asked him how killing the Baker kid could be worse than that? I wanted him to give me absolution."

"*You* confessed–and he absolved you?" Rita said.

"He was a priest. He told me to pray for my eternal soul."

"He tried to get you to confess," Pops said.

"He tried. I just couldn't see the point of it. I was done with 'Nam, done with the army, done with my old man. I had a girl. We were going to get married. I wanted a chance to live a normal life–for once."

"And Sean Nolan?" Pops asked. "Was that an accident too?"

Stan's twitch had stopped. He was crying soundlessly, tears streamed down his face but his words never wavered. "I couldn't believe he had that knife, that it really had been in that shed all those years. I was so wasted when the whole thing went down, I forgot all about it. When I remembered, I wanted to go back and look, but they'd found the kid by that time. There was no way I was going near that shed. Taking the chance of being seen."

"So you killed Sean Nolan because he had the bad luck of finding it?" Rita asked. "Another innocent boy?"

"I offered to buy it off him, tried to con him out of it. Then I told him I knew whose it was and he'd better hand it over, or I'd hand him over to the cops. He wasn't buying any of what I was selling. He got away from me and took off on his bike. He kept looking back to see if I was following. I saw him take that nosedive. I was going to just take the knife and get out of there, I swear. I figured maybe he wouldn't tell—lose face with his buddies and catch hell for not turning it over in the first place when he knew exactly what it was."

"So what happened?"

"He said he knew who the knife belonged to, too, and what I'd done. I knew then that he was going to talk. I couldn't let that happen."

Stan sat up straight in the chair, leaning against the back. He lifted the gun up from the table. "Stan. Don't do something else you're going to regret," Pops said.

Rita reached into her purse for her phone. Her hand was trembling.

Stan shook his head, a slight back and forth motion. "No more. No more regrets." He put the end of the barrel under his chin.

"Stan. Please, don't. Listen to me," Pops said. "I'm begging you. Don't do this. I'll help you. We'll straighten this out."

"It's too late."

Pops was sinking to his knees, pleading with his nephew. "It's not too late, Stan. Let me help you. Please give me the gun." He reached out with both hands, wrapping them around Stan's, holding the gun.

A shot exploded in the small apartment. It was deafening, louder than anything Rita could have ever imagined. Pops gasped and fell back to the floor, clutching his chest. In a flash, Rita was kneeling beside him.

A white powdery dust fell all around them like soft snow, but it was gritty and cut into the skin of her knees. Plaster—it was plaster. She looked up at the ceiling. A bullet hole.

"He's having a heart attack." Stan was yelling at her, but his voice sounded distant, muffled. "He accidentally pulled the trigger when he fell."

She looked back down at Pops. He was still clutching at his chest, moaning in pain.

"Pops!" She was unbuttoning his shirt, still looking for a wound. "Pops, you're going to be okay. You're going to be okay," she kept repeating.

Stan was out of the chair and crouching on the other side of Pops, reaching into his pockets. "It's his heart. He's having a heart attack. Where's his nitro?"

"In his pocket," Rita said. "It's always in his pocket."

Stan found the tiny brown glass bottle in the front pocket of Pops's pants. He unscrewed the lid and shook out a handful of pills, barely specks on his palm. He put one under Pops's tongue.

Rita scrambled for her purse. She dumped the contents on the floor and grabbed her phone, quickly dialing 9-1-1. "I need an ambulance, right now. My grandfather is having a heart attack. Immaculate Heart Senior Residence. Hurry! Please hurry."

She dropped the phone and laid her head on Pops chest. It was barely moving. "Please, Pops. Please don't die." She sat up and looked at Stan. "Give him another pill."

"I think he's supposed to wait fifteen minutes."

"He'll be dead in fifteen minutes. Give him a pill, now." Rita commanded.

"Pops's strained voice was barely a whisper. She leaned closer, putting a shell-shocked ear to his lips.

"I'm sorry, Rita—little Gila girl. I love you."

"No. No, don't you do that. Don't you say goodbye."

He struggled to continue. "So proud of you—always. You'll be just fine."

"Pops, please! Save your strength." She held his hand tight in both of hers.

He reached over and held fast with his other hand. "You. You solved the case. Gave me back my boy."

"Pops, I didn't."

"Yes, you. I believed the worst. You wouldn't give up."

Yes, she wouldn't give up, wouldn't let it go, and now Pops might die. "Pops, don't talk anymore. Save your strength."

Without releasing their intertwined hands, Pops pointed a weak finger toward the ceiling. His gaze shifted to Uncle Stan. "Good thing there's no more floors above, Stan. You might have hurt somebody."

"Pops, you need to save your strength," Rita said again.

"Tell them it was me . . ." His breath rattled in his chest. "Not Stan. Me."

"Pops, you're talking crazy. You don't know what you're saying." Rita could hear the sirens coming from a distance. "You hear that? The ambulance is almost here. Just hang on."

It sounded to her like the entire fleet of Superior police and fire department vehicles were responding. Reflections from their pulsing lights hit the windowpanes in the apartment and chased across the walls.

Pops squeezed her hand. "I'm not going to make it, Rita." His voice was no more than a whisper. "Tell them. Tell—it was me."

Rita felt his grip loosening. He closed his eyes.

"No. No!" she wailed. "Don't you give up, Pops. Do you hear me? Don't you dare give up." She rose up on her knees, placing both hands on his chest, pumping down with all her force, willing her grandfather to draw breath into his lungs with each forceful push. "Breathe, breathe, breathe," she kept repeating.

"Oh God. What have I done?" Stan was sitting on the other side of Pops, cross-legged, looking up at the hole in the ceiling, or maybe the heaven he thought was beyond there, beyond his reach.

"Get up!" Rita yelled at him. "Open the door so they know which apartment we're in."

Two uniforms were the first off the elevator with their guns drawn. Reports of gunshots fired took precedence over the medical emergency. Uncle Stan hit the deck, face down with his hands behind his head.

Rita continued the compressions until the EMTs got the all clear from police to enter the apartment. Pops had no pulse, no blood pressure. They hit him with the portable defibrillator three times before pronouncing him dead.

The apartment was overrun by cops. They talked into their radios and the radios crackled back, but Rita couldn't force her brain to make sense of any of the words. Uncle Stan stood off to the side, alternately confessing his sins and wailing into his hands, cuffed at the wrists.

Rita would remember the moment much as Dali might have captured it on canvas, in bright, garish pigments juxtaposing the grave reality against a ludicrous composition. Her grandfather's face was a frozen mask of death, his arm up in the air—horribly and impossibly—with a finger pointing to a gaping hole in the ceiling that opened to a scene in heaven. Rita's father and Grandma Abby looked down through it. Uncle Stan was a court jester in the corner, his stomach splayed open with his guts spilled out. Robotic police with heads like giant eyeballs and ears like wings recorded the facts in their tiny notebooks.

Later, when Rita had to relate the last moments of Pops's life to Aunt Sue, she left out all the surreal imagery, but she did tell her aunt the part about Pops giving Stan crap about shooting the ceiling. *Tell them it was me.*

"Just like Pops," Sue said. "Always trying to make light of the worst situations."

Of course, that's not what Pops had meant at all. But what difference did it make? Her grandfather was dead because she just had to get her story. With *that* already on her conscience, she didn't feel a whole lot more guilt about not carrying out his dying wish to take the blame for Stan.

XIX

Rita sat back in her chair, swiveling from side to side looking around the small *Telegram* office–much smaller than the old one on Ogden Avenue. She couldn't believe they'd moved to this location more than a year ago. It seemed a much shorter time than that.

Most of the staff hadn't come in for the day yet and her editor was out chasing down a story. The early morning quiet was calming, and the last few weeks had been anything but. She leaned her head back, closed her eyes, and imagined herself soaking up the feeling of stillness, as if it were something that could be held in reserve. But thoughts of the weeks ahead of her urged her to stop dawdling and get on with what needed to be done.

Rita opened her eyes and lifted her head. She ran her hand over the smooth metal desktop, cleared of everything but a computer. She let her fingers slide off the edge. Catching the center drawer handle, she slowly pulled it toward her, feeling the glide of the ball bearing track as the drawer slid open. Carefully arranged pens, pencil, clips, sticky-note pads, and scratch paper occupied the divided sections.

It was all so neat, so prosaic, so uncommitted. The telltale odds and ends that had branded the drawer as hers were gone. Gum and mints, energy bars, a nail file and clear polish, her collection of mismatched dice– all of it in a box at her feet, everything tossed in, landing on top of a few framed photos and favorite books.

She closed the drawer and opened the one to the right. A folded edition of the paper sat on top of the city directory. Rita's editor wrote the breaking news of the Baker and Nolan cases both being solved with one arrest–after a voluntary confession prompted by the paper's investigative reporting. Pops's obituary ran in the same edition on page six.

A soft click broke the silence in the office. Rita looked up to see Rick coming through the front door. She tore the page with the obituary down the center crease, then folded the sheaf carefully and tucked it into the box at her feet. She tossed the rest of the edition into the wastebasket.

Rick walked slowly over to her desk. "Hi," he said, setting down a large cup of coffee from Kwik Trip. "Columbian, no cream, no sugar."

"Thanks." Rita took the cup, popping off the lid to cool the coffee down a bit.

"How's it feel to be back at your desk?" he asked.

"Actually, I came in last night, to clean up my files, put things to bed."

He looked at the box on the floor.

"That's the last of it, then?"

"That's it. Not much for sixteen years."

"No second thoughts?"

Rita took a deep breath. The peace of the nearly deserted office was gone. "We've covered all this Rick. I've turned in my resignation."

"It wasn't your fault, Rita. You have to stop thinking that."

"It is my fault. I couldn't let it go. I had to have the story, and now Pops is dead and Uncle Stan will spend the rest of his life in prison. But that's not why I'm leaving."

Rick stared at her. She felt her jaw clench and her stomach tightened as if expecting a blow. She knew he wanted to say more, wanted to take one last shot at convincing her she had a future here, that *they* had a future—if she would only be patient a little longer. Relief swept over her when he remained silent.

"What's that?" she asked, pointing to a manila envelope Rick had tucked under his arm.

"I promised I'd bring you this after the sentence hearing," he said.

It was a transcript of Uncle Stan's full confession. She'd already heard it, but she wanted the hard copy. She opened the envelope and read over the transcript, fast, remembering the sound of Stan saying the words, tired and spent and ready to be done with it all.

He admitted to killing both Thomas Baker and Sean Nolan, offering enough details to leave no room for doubt, including cutting off Baker's ear. Only he and Rita knew he'd lied when he said he took the ear back to 'Nam with him. There wasn't a single mention of Pops, no hint of any cover-up. As for the knife, Stan did exactly what he'd suggested in the park: After he took it from Sean Nolan, he tossed it off the Bong Bridge. Nobody would ever see it again.

Rita never told Rick about Pops's cover-up, or any of the details she'd heard that night in Uncle Stan's apartment. That would get locked up with Stan and rest in the grave with Pops.

She looked up from the papers to Rick studying her. They lingered on each other's eyes for a moment. Then he asked, "Have you decided where you're going?"

"I've gotten some job offers," she said. "Madison, Chicago, and a few others." She shook her head. "I don't know. I'm looking at some online publications, maybe a managing editor's gig." The relative anonymity of working virtually felt safe to her for now.

Once the story ran in the *Telegram* and the *News Tribune*, it got picked up by the wire services. Cable network lackeys were leaving voicemails with the police department, the DA, Rita's editor, and Rita. She'd even heard a rumor that HBO was considering a movie, but nobody had called her about that.

"Couldn't you work for some online outfit from right here in Superior?"

"I can't stay, Rick. I'm sorry, but I just can't stay here."

"So where are you going?"

Rita added the transcript to her little stash of personal belongings, picked the box off the floor, and stood up. "Wherever the weather is right for my bug," she said. "You've got my number." She kissed him on the cheek and walked out of the *Telegram* office for the last time.

It was still quiet outside. The morning traffic wouldn't pick up for another hour. Rita slid into the driver's seat of the bug, dropping her purse and the box onto the passenger seat beside her.

She'd already cleared her apartment out, selling or donating most of her furnishings. Whatever wouldn't fit into her tiny car she didn't really need. A plastic wastebasket was on the floor in front of the passenger seat, holding a clump of iris she'd dug up from the flowerbed outside the apartment.

She looked at it sitting there now, fragile and ready to tip over. She twisted in the seat again to move her box down to the floor next it, keeping it propped up for all the curves in the road ahead. "Looks like it's just you and me, Charlie," she said to the car—her biggest, most solid possession. "Unless I can find a cat who likes to ride shotgun with a crazy lady at the wheel."

Rita pulled out and headed down Tower Avenue, following the curve onto 3rd street and the approach to the High Bridge. The sun was just coming up over the water, coloring the sky with bold brushstrokes of purple and orange. The dark skyline of Superior stayed visible in her rearview mirror for most of the way across the bridge.

Author's Note

On a summer morning in 1966, fourteen-year old Michael Fisher set out on his paper route in Superior, Wisconsin. Later the same day, his body was found in a ditch. But no killer ever was.

Sins of the Fathers is set in Superior, my childhood home, and it also begins with a cold case from fifty years ago. It was inspired by the actual unsolved murder of Michael Fisher. My fictional Thomas Baker is a boy of about the same age, and it appears that there really was just one desk sergeant on duty the evening Fisher's body was found. But that's as far as the connection goes. Pops is 100% fictional, as is everything else in this little novel of mine, a product of my imagination after a lifetime in this "big town and a small town all in one."

Of course there are *places* that are real and will be familiar to local readers–the hilariously named Bong and High bridges, for example. Setting a story in a particular location necessarily involves using real names of well-known places there. I also used the real name of the *Superior Telegram* newspaper, but only to remind readers that we still have a local paper deserving of our business. Every single reference I make to the *Telegram* is fictional other than its name–the editor, the story snippets, even its entirely fictional reporter Rita Sullivan. In some cases, I deliberately avoided using a real name for a place, as with my fictional Immaculate Heart cathedral.

When it comes to people, it's more difficult to do that, and I didn't try. It's impossible to write fiction without accidentally using some real person's name. There are just too many people out there for me to avoid that while still naming my characters the way parents in places like Superior have named their kids in decades past. To any actual Rita Sullivans, Ricks, Stans, Father Jims, or David Sullivans (or, heaven forbid, even David *Michael* Sullivans) out there, the match between your name and my character's name is entirely, completely coincidental. It certainly isn't you I wrote about. But I hope you enjoy the book just the same.

I am grateful to many people for the help they provided in bringing this book to publication. First to my husband Steve, for always believing in me. Your constant and unconditional support is without equal. To Kay Coletta, who passed away a few short months before I could put a copy in her hands–she set the bar. To Maria Lockwood and Ed Anderson for technical advice, and Teddie Meronek for key pieces of Superior history and lore. To

Chuck Shingledecker for helping me to navigate the publishing process *and* find a great publisher. To my first round editor, Juliana parks and finally, editor and publisher Ed Suominen. Thank you, all.

—Judith Liebaert

33843992R00098

Made in the USA
Middletown, DE
29 July 2016